"Dying To Be Beautiful"
MYSTERY SERIES

BOOK 2: FASHION QUEEN

Joyce,

Thank you for
support and friendship,

Marc

M. GLENDA ROSEN

ISBN: 978-1-4834-4915-9 (sc)
ISBN: 978-1-4834-4914-2 (e)

Because of the dynamic nature of the Internet, any web addresses or links contained in this book may have changed since publication and may no longer be valid. The views expressed in this work are solely those of the author and do not necessarily reflect the views of the publisher, and the publisher hereby disclaims any responsibility for them.

Any people depicted in stock imagery provided by Thinkstock are models, and such images are being used for illustrative purposes only.
Certain stock imagery © Thinkstock.

Lulu Publishing Services rev. date: 04/15/2016

Monday, 6:45 A.M.

Kevin Larson swam in his pool nearly every morning. Going on sixty-five, he prided himself on being in good shape.

Walking toward the small pool house, he noticed a light was on to the left of the pool. He was certain he turned it off the night before. Strange, he thought.

Even stranger, lying in a different sort of pool—blood—was his longtime friend and lover, fashion designer Andre Yellen.

Yellen was stuffed into one of the gowns he had designed and wearing a blond wig. The gown had been auctioned off the night before at a huge Hampton fundraiser.

People in The Hamptons were certainly dying to be beautiful.

CHAPTER 1

THE GOWN

Monday, 7:30 A.M.

Detective Troy Johnson was at Larson's house when Jenna arrived. He had covered the victim with a large beach towel until the coroner and forensics arrived. [deleted "He and"] Sergeant Stan Miller, who had taken the call, accompanied him and was presently attempting to hold back the media. They had heard about Yellen's death on the police scanner, and in no time, the active crime scene was quite a wild sight.

It was 6:30 A.M. when she had received the call from Johnson that he was on his way to Kevin Larson's house: "Jenna, there's been a murder. Designer Andre Yellen, the Fashion Queen, was found dead this morning at the home of movie mogul Kevin Larson. He gave her the address and exactly where it was located, "past the windmill at the edge of Southampton."

"More like the situation was at the edge of reason," Jenna thought.

"Jenna, they're acting like a bunch of hungry vultures. Help! These are your people. Well, they're reporters like you used to be. The homeowner is either in shock or just completely uncooperative except for telling me where and when he found Yellen's body."

Jenna sighed, "Sure, I can't say no to such a lovely invitation."

The death of Andre Yellen was big news.

1

Andre Yellen was squeezed—really, truly squeezed—into a beautiful ocean blue, sleeveless, silk gown he had designed and donated for a fundraiser the evening before. The size-8 dress was torn at all the seams. Yellen, in his early fifties, 5'9" and clearly out of shape, was more like a size-18-plus, and stuffed into a dress way, way too small for him.

As a designer for major celebrities for nearly twenty-five years, Yellen was a man about town who loved both the ladies and the men, or so it had been gossiped around the East End of Long Island, also known as The Hamptons.

After all, this *is* THE HAMPTONS, and all sorts of lifestyles are accepted, where choices are supposedly not judged, and relationships are not restricted by conventional boundaries. Unfortunately, there are always those determined to exercise their own brand of severe judgment.

However, there was no evidence this murder had anything to do with narrow minds. Not yet, anyhow. In fact, it wasn't clear at all what this murder was about—or who had committed it.

Private Investigator Jenna Preston was familiar with many celebrities who lived or vacationed on the East End. Before becoming an investigative reporter, she was entertainment and social events reporter for the local daily paper and had interviewed quite a few of the "anointed" as she had once called them. Gossip columnists covered the rest.

Jenna was regularly hired by law firms, insurance companies and businesses for corporate fraud issues. She also had an arrangement and relationship with the local police—especially when it came to murder investigations. Some of the people she had once written about also tried to hire her for personal investigations and for, what she considered, ridiculous reasons. Such complaints included some new fence being too high or people walking on the beach in front of someone's home.

Most of these cases she didn't accept.

"For me, it's about justice. We all have reasons, even life experiences motivating our passions. I have mine for what I do," Jenna told a local reporter whose paper was doing a story on crime in The Hamptons.

Jenna had a solid reputation for being smart, resourceful and most definitely charming—without an attitude—which was different from many of the people who summered in The Hamptons.

She did love nice clothes, including the red shoes or red boots she almost always wore.

"Hey," she laughed once when Troy made fun of her red shoes, "you wear a cowboy hat most of the time, so don't make fun of me, Tex."

Jenna and Troy worked together professionally almost as soon as she had become a licensed private detective. It was a small police force, often stretched thin during the summer season. Because they actually had few experienced investigators, he had requested and been given approval by his captain to use a discretionary fund to hire Jenna on an as-needed basis. She was often a member of his investigative team, usually for murders.

Lately, there didn't seem to be any shortage of them.

Slender and almost 5'5," yet always looking taller in her two or three inch heels, Jenna had long red hair, sometimes pulled back in a ponytail when she was working. She also had deep blue eyes. With more than a hint of spunk and mischief about her, she was definitely considered attractive.

Jenna's new romance, Dave, thought so!

***

So, here she was involved in another murder scene in this enclave of the wealthy and famous—and those who wanted to hang out with them. Each year the entire East End became a chaotic place during the summer months, which was known as "the season."

The season that was once three months a year is now five months long, thanks to technology people who could run their businesses—in fact, much of their lives—from their beach homes. On any given weekend, there are a dozen fundraising events dedicated to a hospital building, a new healthcare center or an emergency wing, all named after wealthy patrons. Lately, some of the most popular events are devoted to animal shelters.

It has been repeatedly remarked that people out here would give away their children more easily than their dogs or cats! Some of these summer fundraising events cost upwards of $500 per person to attend and are a financial boon for caterers, party planners, entertainers and fashion designers.

Much of the natural beauty of the East End remains, although somewhat compromised by huge homes along pristine beaches that are at times closed off to day-trippers "in season."

Much to the chagrin of many wealthy homeowners, and even some of the locals, the past couple of years brought in droves of youth from New Jersey who had lost their own playground beaches to Hurricane Sandy. They had landed on the shores of The Hamptons with loud music, beer parties and free-for-all sex. Well, anyhow that was what the complaints to the police said.

Year-round residents tolerated the summer people, barely, especially if they owned businesses that benefited from the excessive amounts of money they spent on landscaping, pool maintenance, house-cleaning services, and dining out at high priced restaurants.

Fashion and being fashionable were a major influence on life and parties throughout the summer in The Hamptons. Designers, high-end retailers and attractive male and female models were all part of the show. Fashion was fun. It was also a business of fierce competition and extravagance. Fashionable people faced endless demands to spend a great deal of money in an effort to look fabulous.

Jenna stared at the body of Andre Yellen with its rolls of fat sticking out from the torn seams, his dead face bloated. "This is damn freaky, Troy. How the hell did they even get this gown on him? Wearing a one-of-a-kind Andre Yellen gown at a big annual event out here is like winning an Oscar."

It sure as hell wasn't intended for this occasion.

***

Jenna, once described her own fashion style, "It's sort of like Kathryn Hepburn's, casual and classic, except I don't exactly have her long, lean look."

Jenna's relationship with Troy, that is, Detective Troy Johnson, began as a summer fling. They were now close friends as they had worked together on quite a few criminal cases over the past five years; more so in the summer when the craziness increased significantly.

Jenna had explained her career change to Dave: "I was politely asked to leave the paper as an investigative reporter because our area senator pretty much threatened to sue the paper for a story I had written about a couple of well-to-do residents. *They* of course had donated lots of money to his campaigns. Even though the story was true, and they were eventually arrested for murder and acts of indecent behavior against minors, the paper didn't want to chance a lawsuit, let alone a problem with the senator. Money people put him in office and made him influential as long as he did what they wanted him to do on their behalf."

"Well, I have influential connections, too," Jenna told Troy as she was walking Watson, having already explained to Troy why the paper had fired her.

Troy commiserated with Jenna and agreed with her conclusion. "I know you have many valuable connections on the East End, and of course, there are your prominent parents in Manhattan."

Troy reminded her that he also had some darn good local connections. "I know many of the locals, and they often know where the bodies are hidden, so to speak. They know who hangs out where; if they're gambling, drinking, doing drugs, having affairs. We do make a great team, Jenna Preston!"

That they did!

Jenna had gotten her private investigator license over five years ago and then opened Watson Discreet Investigations. When she got her Irish setter, she also named him Watson.

"It makes me happy to call him Watson. I love Sherlock Holmes mysteries. His books and stories offer so much insight into human behavior, and, well, he just wouldn't be Holmes without Watson. So, I eventually figured I needed a Watson to help me."

***

Jenna climbed over beach towels strewn around Larson's pool to get to Detective Johnson. The blood was now covering a good-size area around the pool. Some of the towels apparently were from people who had been swimming there the previous day. They were still damp. Several of them were spread out to soak up some of the blood in an attempt to keep it from going into the pool.

Jenna moved closer to the body. She saw it was dressed in a gown that must have been beautiful before it was stretched onto this dead body. He was also wearing a blond wig.

Jenna teased Detective Johnson about the press out front. With a glint in her eye, knowing how much he hated dealing with the media, she said, "You know this is about to be a three-ring circus. They are already camping out front. No wonder you wanted me here to protect you from them. Welcome to summer in The Hamptons!"

Two television reporters had set up their cameras. One was from a national network. Local radio and newspaper reporters were vying for the best location in an attempt to get interviews. The daily and weekly Hampton rags were begging for an opportunity to take photos. Everyone had been told they would have to wait.

"Listen, it's a crime scene in there," Sergeant Miller had been telling the media. "You'll have to wait. Please be patient, and someone will come out and give you an update as soon as possible."

"Jenna, after Doc and Lara are done here and the body is removed to the coroners lab, *please* do me a favor. Tell the media we will have a statement for them later this afternoon, maybe around 3 P.M. at police headquarters. However, for now, 'No comment.'"

"Of course, Detective Johnson! But you'll owe me," Jenna grinned.

Doc Bishop, the local coroner, and Lara Stern, head of the forensic crime lab for the entire East End of Long Island, came through the back gate of the house. Doc and his assistant, as usual, someone young, helped him bring in the gurney to collect the body.

Bending over the body, Doc looked up, "Detective, this guy didn't get murdered here. Check out the bottom of his bare feet. He was dragged here. I can be more specific about how he was murdered and why so much blood loss when we get him back to the morgue. Rigor mortis is setting in. His body is cold and from his temperature, I would say he's been dead about four to six hours."

Troy bent down to look at the scrape marks on Yellen's feet. He had to have been killed where there was some mud or dirt, which was left on the bottom of his feet.

"This might help us figure out where the murder happened," Troy suggested.

"Jenna is going to hold off the media for us, 'No comment' for now. We'll set up a press conference for later this afternoon when we might in fact have some news for them. That gives us some time to have you give us an idea of what really happened to him."

"Plus this gown, which is probably worth at least $10,000, is ripped from being dragged. Well, and from being a lot too small for his rather stout frame," Jenna commented as she bent over the body next to Troy.

"We need to get the gown off him at the lab so we can check it for any evidence. Maybe it'll give us some other clues,"

Jenna put on a pair of gloves, reached over the body and pulled off the wig. "This wig looks like it came from a costume shop. It's really cheap. The black polish on his thumbnails may have come from a local drugstore, although it doesn't look like any type of nail polish I've ever seen before."

Jenna knew they would also check for bruises and rape. It was part of processing the dead who had been murdered. Lovely, she thought, shaking her head to the three of them. "Here lies a multi-million dollar fashion designer, in a ten-dollar wig, cheap nail polish and looking like a hooker. I would imagine someone intended on making a statement, dressing him up like this."

"It's possible he's been sexually assaulted," Troy was pointing to some bruises on his body.

"Could be a motive. I'll let you know," replied Doc, getting up and calling the intern to bring the gurney over to the body.

"Let's get him out of here and see what you two can find out. Jenna and I will meet both of you at the coroner's office later." Troy got up and looked over at Kevin Larson, who was clearly distraught. As the owner of the house where Yellen had been found murdered, Larson had to be a prime suspect.

The house was spectacular, painted all white except for dark magenta trim around the windows that were almost all floor-to-ceiling downstairs with smaller ones upstairs. The paths to the front and back of the house were lined with all sorts of trees and other flora, surely managed by professionals. The pool house matched the main house except it had only a few small windows with magenta miniblinds so people could change in private into or out of their swimwear (or possibly use the pool house for other private activities). It was on an acre of prime property only blocks from the ocean.

"I want to have another conversation with Kevin Larson. Jenna, if you wouldn't mind, give Patricia Tilton at the paper a call. See what she has on Yellen and Larson," said Troy as he was walking toward Larson.

Patricia, the senior editor for local news at the daily paper, was a friend of Jenna's since they had worked at the same paper and she was a damn good reliable source of information regarding life and gossip on the East End.

"Patricia, it's Jenna. Call me as soon as possible. You probably heard Andre Yellen was found murdered by Kevin Larson's pool. Detective Johnson and I are hoping you can give us some background information on both of them. Can you check out what might have been in the paper about them in the last couple of years? If possible, let's meet at the Burger Bar for lunch, any time after 12:30."

The Burger Bar was the popular in-place for locals. They loved that the rich found it too seedy for them with its plastic chairs, burgers served in plastic baskets and drinks in large plastic cups. But, oh, the food was so good with many-generations-old recipes kept secret to this day!

Jenna looked out to see who was in the crowd. She turned back to watch Doc and his intern zip Yellen into the body bag and then supervise it being carried to the medical van. It would soon be on its way to being sliced, probed and explored from head to toe.

Not a pretty end for the Fashion Queen, as Yellen was known.

As Yellen was being carried out, Jenna turned to Troy, "His clothing is often featured in high-end fashion and society magazines, plus there are plenty of photos of the rich wearing them at parties, weddings and, of course, fundraising events. We need to take a look at some of the more recent photos. I'll see what Patricia and I can find."

The growing media presence was camped out on Larson's massive front lawn. More television cameras, radio reporters and local newspapers had arrived. This was big news. Andre Yellen was a big name in fashion all over the world. Jenna went out to talk to them, nodded to a few she knew, "Detective Johnson said he has 'no comment' at this time on the death of Andre Yellen," Jenna told them.

"He expects to make a statement and possibly answer questions later this afternoon at police headquarters, probably around 3 or 4 P.M.

Sergeant Miller, the department's communication director, will text you later with the exact time.

The crowd shouted: "Was he murdered? Do you know who did this? Where is Kevin Larson?"

Jenna started to walk back inside without answering, when a young male television reporter grabbed at her, pleading, "I need to get inside to get this on television."

"That's not going to happen. The body is going to the morgue very soon."

Back by the pool, while waiting for Troy to finish *trying* to get more information from Larson, she noticed the side wall of the pool house was covered with an odd color stream of moisture.

Jenna called Lara over. "Can you check out what in the world is this on the side wall here?"

"Semen."

"Damn, Lara, how did you figure that out right away?"

"The joys of forensic investigation," Lara laughed, and Jenna called Detective Johnson over.

"Here, take a look. Someone began or ended this murder with a personal pleasure!" Jenna stepped aside while Troy took a look. He walked around the entire pool house, inside and out, while Lara began bagging evidence including samples of the semen, blood and pieces of material that had been ripped off from the gown

"Larson, what do you know about this?" Johnson got him up from the chair he had been sitting on near his pool patio. He was wearing shorts, a t-shirt and sandals. He had his hands folded under his chin, tears in his eyes.

Kevin Larson was in his sixties with a full head of grey hair, slender and about 5'11". His nose was slightly crooked, giving his face a sense of being almost good-looking, but not quite. In some of his photos in the papers, he looked rather sinister, according to Jenna and Troy. They reached that conclusion later in the day after Patricia had emailed the articles to the station.

"My attorney is on his way." This was Larson's only comment before he pulled his arm away from the detective and went inside his 'beautiful' multi-million dollar house. Now, a crime scene!

CHAPTER 2

MISSING

Before Jenna arrived at the crime scene, Troy had already found out which event Yellen was at the night before and who was the head of the event. He also learned that the gown Yellen was wearing had been donated to that same event and who had won the winning bid for the dress. All this from a local weekly paper reporter he had known for many years who had cozied up to him and politely begged him to be allowed to take at least one photo of the dead Yellen, killed wearing his own dress! Troy gave him three minutes, then pushed him back into the crowd of reporters, onlookers and television cameras.

Sergeant Miller had also taken photos of the crime scene. "Detective, I'll get these photos ready for you once I can leave here."

The media attention was growing. Word spread quickly when celebrities were involved, be it in marriage or murder. This was more than Hamptons news. It was national news.

Meantime, Sergeant Stan Miller had taken an urgent call for Detective Johnson. The Sergeant whispered to Detective Johnson so the onslaught of media couldn't hear him, "A Nora Flynn called, hysterical. Said she was mugged, drugged and robbed of the Andre Yellen gown. She had had the winning bid for it last night at a hospital fundraiser."

"Thanks, Stan, and stay here until Lara is finished collecting evidence so the reporters don't trample her to death in the process. Plus, be sure to keep the crime scene tape up around the house and entrance to the pool area. I'll call headquarters to get another officer out here to relieve you so we can get those photos made."

"Sure. By the way, Nora Flynn is not aware Yellen's dead. I figure you can break the news to her."

"Good thinking. We'll see how she responds when we tell her in person."

The sergeant handed the detective the address he had written in his note pad, "I told her you would be there soon. She sounds scared and frantic. Said she doesn't remember how she ended up lying on her living room floor. Maybe she can shed some light on what happened to Yellen."

Detective Johnson took the address, then pulled Jenna aside and told her about the call from Nora Flynn. "Want to come with me?"

Like he could keep her away.

Meantime, Patricia Tilton left a message she would meet Jenna at the Burger Bar at 12:30. "It's huge! You have no idea how everyone is going nuts over this story."

Jenna followed Troy to Nora's house, curious about this newest wrinkle in the 'gown'. "I know," she said to herself, "not so funny."

***

They found Nora Flynn in a state of near hysteria. Sobbing, waiting outside by a lawn that had more weeds that grass, she called to them to come inside. Pretty, slightly chubby, light brown hair and maybe a little under 5'2." Nora looked a mess with tears streaming down her face of day-old makeup. She was wearing a wrinkled t-shirt and too tight jeans.

"The inside of Nora's house didn't look any better," Jenna thought as she went inside to an even worse mess. Nora Flynn was not a tidy housekeeper. Week-old papers were strewn about along with empty cans of cola and beer, a pizza box and even a cup that held cigarette ashes—from someone else's cigarette, they later learned.

"Nora, I'm Detective Johnson. This is Jenna Preston, a private investigator who works with our police department. We need to ask you some questions. Please, we need you to sit down, and tell us what you remember about last night."

Detective Johnson was making notes, standing in front of Nora. Jenna sat on the worn, dark brown sofa next to her.

Nora couldn't seem to sit still. She crossed and uncrossed her legs, wiped tears from her eyes, tried to smoke a cigarette, then put it out.

"Some lady, I think the auction chair, gave me the gown before I left. She had put it in a plastic garment bag. I put it over my arm and went to my car. I drove right home, and when I went to unlock my door, someone came up behind me and put their hand over my mouth. It felt like my arm was stuck with a needle and next thing I knew, I woke up on my living room floor," Nora said, and then began sobbing uncontrollably.

"Could you tell if it was a man or a women who attacked you?"

"A man, I think, someone tall. Well, almost anyone feels tall to me. I'm kinda short."

"Did you see him even for a split second, maybe recognize anything about them?"

"Not really, it was dark when I got home. The front light is broken so it was hard to see anything. I think I noticed, from the arm that came around my face, the person was wearing something black."

Jenna looked at Troy because she had a couple of questions. He nodded for her to go ahead.

"Was there anything you could recognize, the smell of tobacco or perfume? Large or small hands of a man or woman?"

"Perfume, cologne. I'm not sure what, but I would know it if I smelled it again. Almost sweet smelling."

"When you woke up inside, were you dressed in the same clothes you wore last night?" Jenna looked up at Troy. He knew she was trying to find out if Nora might have been raped.

"Yes, of course. It took me a few minutes to get up. I was confused. I couldn't figure out what happened. Then, I saw the empty garment bag and realized the gown was gone. That's when I called the police. That gown is worth a lot of money."

"What were you wearing last night? I assume you changed before we got here." Nora nodded yes to Jenna and went into her bedroom. She brought out a pale pink, short satin dress probably bought at a bargain somewhere, but Nora Flynn clearly loved the dress.

"I bought this to wear last night . . . with some of the money Mr. Yellen gave me. It was all wrinkled when I woke up on the floor, so I took it off before you got here."

"Nora, we're going to need to take the dress with us to see if there is any evidence on it. We'll get it back to you when we're done with it."

Handing the cheap pink dress to Troy, she held on to it for a minute longer; the hesitation saying so much about her and—what seemed to Jenna—the poor woman's somewhat deprived and empty life.

Troy stood up and walked around her living room, looking at the small, rather untidy kitchen, and wondered aloud, "Nora, how could you afford the winning bid on that gown?"

Shaking and unresponsive, Nora sat with her head in her hands. Jenna and Troy both realized she never could have bought that expensive gown on her own.

Jenna tried to be reassuring to open her up: "Nora, it's okay if you had bid on it for someone else. People do that all the time out here."

Well, what's a little white lie in a murder case!

Troy was firmer and went for the shock response. "We need to know who asked you to bid on that gown, Nora, or I'll have to take you to police headquarters now. This morning, Andre Yellen was found stuffed into that gown and murdered, and the last person known to have it is you. I need some answers from you." The detective was now leaning over Nora, pushing her into telling what she knew.

"What are you talking about?" Nora Flynn looked like she had just been hit over the head. Her response of shock seemed real. Her sobbing began again, and she ran into the kitchen to throw cold water on her face.

Walking back into the living room she practically whispered. "It can't be, I spoke to him last night. I sat with him. I didn't kill him. I didn't kill him. I couldn't, I couldn't kill him. He was the one who paid me to bid on the gown. I was supposed to give it back to him when I got home after the event."

Jenna and Troy looked at her. Now they were shocked.

Jenna got up and leaned over her, "Nora, this is serious. Did he tell you why he wanted you to do this for him? We need to know exactly what went on between the two of you, when you made the plans to do this. How much was he paying you?"

Between more tears and gasping sobs, Nora explained how she knew Yellen and how he asked for her help. "We met at Dr. Keller's office. Dr. Christian Keller and his wife, Dr. Alana Keller, were co-chairs for last night's fundraiser. I work for Dr. Christian Keller as his office manager.

"I was flattered that *the* Andre Yellen was being so nice and attentive, after all the negative and hateful comments I heard Dr. Keller say about him to his wife. She's also a doctor with her own office further Out East. I rarely see her."

"Did *the* Doctor Keller you work for know Yellen was acting very friendly to you? Did he warn you about him?" asked Detective Johnson.

Jenna sat down and moved a little closer to Nora, hoping to make her feel less upset. She added in another question that was now nagging at her, "Did Dr. Keller threaten you in any way for your being friendly with Yellen?"

"At first, he cautioned me that Andre Yellen was not a nice man. He explained I should know he couldn't be trusted. I told him we just talked when he had come into the office to see Dr. Keller. That's when Dr. Keller did sort of threaten me. He said I'd better not see Yellen outside of the office or I would lose my job. I was surprised how strongly he felt about this. Then he warned me again that this was a nasty man who would only cause me trouble. I guess he was right, considering what's happening!"

Troy put his notepad in his pocket, looked around Nora's run-down house and said to Jenna, "Why don't you and Nora finish talking. I'm going to check around outside where she said she was attacked. I called Lara Stern to come here and check for evidence, and Sergeant Miller is on his way to put up crime scene tape and take photos."

Miller was outside: "By the way 'Sir' you will be delighted to know the press is headed toward the police station." The sergeant knew Detective Johnson would hardly be delighted.

Jenna knew Troy wanted her to see if she could get more information from Nora. Maybe with him outside, she might talk more freely about her so-called friendship with Yellen.

Jenna asked to use the bathroom as an excuse to take a quick look around Nora's home. It was small with two bedrooms. The bigger one seemed to be Nora's, with her clothes and laundry strewn on the bed and floor. Jenna was only surprised by a display of at least ten pictures in nice frames on a cheap dresser. The older people could be Nora's parents and the others could be from her childhood. There were two boys and a little girl, who was a miniature version of Nora.

The rest of the rooms had unmatched furniture throughout with ashtrays that had been frequently used. Empty soda and beer cans lay on a table in the bedroom. The bathroom and kitchen probably hadn't been adequately cleaned in ages.

Jenna had also noticed Nora's car in the driveway was at least ten years old with several rusting dents in it.

"Nora, how did Andre Yellen explain to you about bidding on his gown for him?"

"After one of his visits with the doctor, he sent me a thank-you note for being so nice to him. He also invited me to have a drink with him, at a kind of out-of-the-way place so it could be private. I know, I'm very gullible, but when someone that rich and famous invites you out, it's hard to say no."

"Where did you meet?"

"We met at the Oyster Bar on the North Fork."

Jenna knew exactly where that was. She and Dave had been there a number of times since it was not far from his place.

Dave Carter's place was twelve beautiful acres on the North Fork, the desire of several architects and builders that wanted to divide it into smaller subdivision parcels for million-dollar homes. Dave's answer was always an emphatic, "No!"

The Oyster Bar was a popular restaurant with great food, but on a Saturday afternoon, few Hampton people would be there. It was, however, a favorite place where Dave and Jenna had dinner all year round.

"Nora," asked Jenna, "really, did you think it was meant to be a romantic meeting?"

"No. I kinda thought he might want my help convincing Dr. Keller to let him donate that gown for the hospital auction. I had heard them screaming each time he came to the office, and it was always about that gown. When we met, he ordered some drinks and food for us. He even apologized for bringing me there on an uncomfortable pretense.

"He explained he had a problem and thought maybe I could help him. I didn't know—I still don't why—he was so desperate to donate it. He's a very famous fashion designer . . . *Was*."

"What did he ask you to do?"

"He said he would pay me one thousand dollars if I could convince the doctor to allow the donation of the gown. I was to go to the event and bid on it until I had the winning bid. He said he would pay for that bid, and afterwards he would pick up the gown from me."

Jenna sat quietly, nodding, listening to her. After taking a deep breath, Nora went on with more of the story. "I know, I thought it sounded crazy and complicated. He said he had a good reason, and it would be a huge help to him. He handed me an envelope with $500 cash and told me I would get the rest when he picked up the gown from me. That's a lot of money for me, so I agreed to help him."

"Weren't you afraid he would know Yellen had been behind it?"

"Not really, I sort of knew how to push Dr. Keller. Dr. Alana Keller was another thorn in his side, and I also knew she wanted the gown donated even less than he did. I heard him screaming and threatening her about it over the phone a couple of weeks ago.

"When I spoke to Dr. Keller later in the day, right after the fight with his wife, I pretended—okay, I lied—that Andre Yellen had left another message about donating his gown for the fundraiser. I kept on talking real fast-like: I said it would raise a lot of money for the event and how I wish I had a Yellen dress.

"Then what happened?" Jenna was getting seriously frustrated and impatient with Nora.

"He shouted at me to call and tell the damn S.O.B., 'Yes.' I did that as soon as Dr. Keller went out to lunch. I thought I should let Mr. Yellen know before the doctor changed his mind, which he never did."

"Mr. Yellen called me right back to say I did a great job and said he would meet with me the day before the event to give me my ticket to attend, and he would tell me how to go about bidding for the gown so I would win. I didn't think much about that until the day before the event, which was this past Saturday. He asked me to meet him that afternoon at the same place we had met before. For another $500, I was willing to do what he asked. It didn't seem like it was anything illegal or dangerous."

"Nora, when you met with him on Saturday, did he tell you why he wanted you to bid on the gown and how much you could bid for it?"

"Oh yes," she told Jenna. "Well, no, not about why. He was very specific about the bid. First, he gave me a ticket to the event—you know they were $450 per person—then he gave me a signed blank check made out to me to buy the gown. He said I should pay for it out of my own checking account and then deposit this one for the same amount into my account to cover it. I was amazed he trusted me like that. Then again, I did have enough sense not to betray him with all his connections and money."

"But Nora, you have no idea why he wanted you to do all this?"

Nora, her face all red and puffy from crying, said, "I asked him why and he refused to tell me. He said it was a very personal matter and since he had come to know me, he believed I could keep his confidence and trust. I realized that wasn't an answer, but I also realized he wasn't going to say any more about it to me."

"What did he do after that?"

"He gave me the ticket and the check. He said to keep going back to the bid table and make my bid higher than any other, until the bidding was over. He said I was to be sure that, when I left, I took the gown with me. Oh, he also gave me the remaining $500 he promised me, in cash, like the first half. I was surprised he gave it to me before the event, but that's how I could buy my pretty pink dress that you took."

Jenna continued questioning Nora, but her every instinct told her she wasn't getting the whole truth—not now, anyhow!

"Was Yellen at the event all evening?" Jenna was getting more and more impatient. She found this young woman annoyingly gullible. She wanted to move this along so she could meet Patricia Tilton at the Burger Bar. Jenna expected that Patricia would have information—as well as plenty of gossip—on the now dead, very flamboyant, Andre Yellen.

Troy had walked back in and listened as Nora told Jenna about the rest of her evening.

"I left close to 10 P.M. Couples started dancing, and since I was there alone and had done what I was paid to do, which is win the bid, I wanted to get the gown, go home and be done with this already."

"Did Yellen see the gown being handed to you?"

"No. He was there the beginning of the evening. He was not there when I left. I assumed he would come to my home before midnight to pick the gown up from me like we had planned. I was directed to a lady who was in charge of the auction. I don't know her name either. I'm sure the doctor will be able to tell you, and as I said, she told me the gown was being wrapped in a garment bag, and I could take it once I gave her the payment. I gave her the check, my ID and waited until she brought me the gown."

"Nora, this is very important, did anyone talk to you about winning the gown or stop you on your way out?"

"Yes."

"Who?"

"I was anxious to leave. I was sure people there wondered how I could bid so high for that gown. As I started to walk out, my boss, Dr. Keller, came toward me as the lady handed me the gown. When she walked away he put his arm around me, real friendly-like, and whispered in my ear, 'You're fired. Now I know why you wanted me to let the crude S.O.B. Yellen donate his gown.'"

"Did the doctor follow you out?"

"No, but he asked me how much Yellen paid me to do this. Then Dr. Keller said: 'Be sure to tell him he won't get away with it. He's going to pay more, much more, than money for doing this.' I turned and went to my car with the gown. I was really upset he was so angry with me."

Jenna stood up and handed Nora her card. "By the way, did you see anyone following you when you left?"

"No, I was kinda nervous about the whole thing and anxious about carrying around such an expensive gown."

"Nora, the police are going to have more questions for you, and Lara Stern, the head of forensics, will be over sometime this afternoon. You're not to leave here until she's done. We'll need you to come to the station later. Sergeant Miller will tell you when to be there."

"Can I call my boyfriend and my brother to come over so I'm not alone?"

"If absolutely necessary," Jenna answered hesitatingly. Something still didn't feel right, but there was not much she could do about it now. "I have a couple more questions for you. Did you have any contact with Dr. Alana Keller at the event or see her arguing with her husband?"

"She never came near me, although I saw her glaring at me when I was handed the gown. The only time I saw the two doctors together was in the reception line at the beginning, never after that."

"What color dress or gown was she wearing?"

"Black. This may sound silly, but when I first saw her in it, I thought the design looked almost like the gown that had been donated by Yellen."

That surprised Jenna, as did much of this interview. She was about to comment, but decided it was best to get this information to Detective Johnson and leave to meet Patricia. There would time for more, later.

Detective Johnson met Jenna outside telling her, "I'll see you this afternoon. I'm on way to the coroners. I've called for a press briefing here at 3:15 P.M. Stan will get Emails and tweets out to all of the vultures."

"Troy, after I meet Patricia, I'll come to the station. I should be by two this afternoon. I have a heck of a lot of what I think is rather odd information from Nora Flynn. She did say Dr. Keller threatened Yellen when she left with the gown last night. Can you ask Lara to also check for any evidence on the clothes Nora was wearing? I told her not to leave until Lara is done checking forensics. I'm not sure about this mugging story. See you later."

In the few minutes of quiet in her car on the way to the Burger Bar, Jenna thought about Nora.

Nora, her boyfriend and her brother, where are they?

And what about the Keller doctors, Kevin Larson and, of course, the Fashion Queen himself, Andre Yellen? Patricia is sure to have 'the goods' on these characters.

The whole situation seemed like an old Hollywood *film noir*. Kevin Larson… years ago, hadn't he produced a couple of those movies?

CHAPTER 3

GOSSIP

By 12:15, Jenna was on her way to meet Patricia. This was sure to be much more enjoyable than her morning at the murder scene and the dramatic conversation with Nora Flynn.

"Andre Yellen slept with both Dr. Kellers and Kevin Larson," Patricia Tilton told Jenna. "This began close to twenty-five years ago. He also slept with any number of fashion models and movie stars, male and female," she smirked. "He was an equal opportunity cad. There have always been many articles about his behavior in the gossip columns and his fashions showed up in all the glamour magazines. There have been plenty of photos of him with big-name celebrities and society people wearing his clothes." Then, Patricia stopped to take a healthy size bite of her "mile-high burger." It was named that for a very good reason.

"Patricia, I'm really curious, if I get you a photo of the gown that was donated last night, can you search to see if anyone has been photographed in it and when? There's something about this particular gown that seems to have created a maelstrom of arguments, screaming, innuendos, and now the designer's murder."

"Was he really stuffed into that gown?"

"Sure was. He was lying next to Larson's pool wearing it, plus he had on a blond wig and black nail polish. One of the local rags managed to get photos of him, plus television crews were out there angling for shots."

"This is already making national news," Patricia told her. "You know, I'll bet his clothes will probably be selling for a small fortune, since he won't be designing anymore."

"Patricia, what else do you know about Larson, particularly in regards to Yellen? Any articles on them, beside their having slept together? Did they have any business dealings with each other, travel anywhere together? There must be something more to his being dumped by Larson's pool."

"I only had a couple of hours to do some checking on it this morning. However, I did find an industry piece regarding their history together. They had been business partners some twenty-five years ago. Yellen was starting to make it big and there were several photos of him with Dr. Keller's arm around him. Keller wasn't married yet."

Jenna set her burger onto the plastic plate. "Patricia, there is much more involved here than any of us know right now. I didn't believe half of what Nora Flynn told us. I'm positive there's a damn lot more to the story since Kevin Larson immediately lawyered up. Of course, we still haven't spoken with either Dr. Keller. We'll have to get to them both as soon as possible. I'm positive they're in the middle of this somehow."

"I agree. There were stories printed about Dr. Christian Keller and Yellen's 'breakup,' both business and personal. Each was suing the other for fraud, for financial mishandling of company funds and ended up in a court fight. Finally there was a big settlement, undisclosed unfortunately. So far, all I came up with from a few of the older stories was that Larson did have some of his film stars wear Yellen's clothes in a couple of his movies. This was maybe ten years ago, maybe longer."

"They are a complex, untrustworthy group of characters living the high life, with much of their summers spent here in The Hamptons the last half-dozen years. Oh, one last bit of gossip—Dr. Alana Keller also apparently slept with both Yellen and Larson even after she was married."

"Really?" Jenna sat back in her chair in the Burger Bar with an expression that said: "You *gotta* be kidding me!"

"Hey, I only report the news," Patricia laughed.

Giving Patricia a chance to take another bite into her burger, Jenna posed the question, "With all their financial mishandlings, I wonder how much money was involved, and if there's any connections to some of the other big players out here?"

"I'm sure there has to be."

"Patricia, one other person I'm curious about, Nora Flynn. She's the young lady who won the bid for Yellen's gown at the fundraiser last night, which was chaired by both Dr. Kellers. I wonder if there might be any photos in the paper of her with any one of these characters."

"Jenna, darling, you need a research assistant!"

"A thought I've had recently. Want the job?

Patricia laughed out loud, immediately attending to the production of eating her burger. Meantime, Jenna filled her in on what Nora Flynn told her earlier; confident she would do a story without any false embellishments. She had a reputation as a damn good reporter. Rewinding that interview in her own mind, she felt that Nora had manipulated pieces of the story and left out other critical pieces of information. Perhaps she had reason to be afraid of her boss, Dr. Christian Keller. She definitely wanted to talk to her again.

As they finished their burgers, Patricia said she planned to have a story on this in the next edition of the paper and promised to let Jenna know what else she found out. "I left my new intern at the paper researching more on these people, including gossip about cheating husbands and wives, especially regarding them. They're likely to have had plenty of that going on."

"Okay, thanks. I'm on my way to meet Detective Johnson at the coroner's. Lara Stern was headed to Nora Flynn's house."

"Jenna, you should definitely check what's been written about any of these people, especially with photos, in the local weekly rags. You know a couple of the publishers. I'm sure they'd be glad to help for an inside scoop on this murder."

"I plan to. In addition to talking to the Kellers, we'll interview Larson, with his attorney most assuredly, and speak more with Nora—this time, at the station. We need to scare her into telling the truth—if that's possible."

***

As she left the Burger Bar, Jenna gave Patricia a hug, another thank you, and a promise to keep her up to date with any breaking news on the case. Then, Jenna went home to feed Watson and bring him with her for the afternoon. She didn't like leaving him alone for too many hours. Well, actually it made her happy to have him with her. Sometimes, she felt like Watson was smiling, especially when he rode in the car and stuck his head out the window letting the breeze blow through his red furry coat.

When he heard Jenna, Watson came bounding in from the backyard, and after a loving welcome and downing his meal in about three seconds; he and Jenna jumped into her jeep and headed into town. Watson had been spending a lot of time at Dave's recently, getting acquainted with his new Irish setter sister. Aggie was staying at Dave's for now or maybe permanently. That depended on if she and Dave got married, a subject also on hold… for now.

Aggie was still very tiny, tripping over her own feet, running around in circles after her own tail. When Watson would let her get near him, Aggie gave him wet kisses. She was not going to be as big as he was, but she sure was adorable. She may not have quite the same energy as Watson either. She seemed to be more mellow than her brother.

Then again, she might learn a few new tricks from Watson.

***

"Troy, I'll be there in ten minutes. Wondering if you've scheduled interviews with any witnesses or suspects?" Jenna asked.

"Not yet. After talking to Doc Bishop, I wanted to discuss his preliminary findings with you, plus I doubt we'll get much from Lara Stern until tomorrow morning. She has a lot of samples for forensics testing. Meantime, before I do the press conference, let's plan how best to split up the interviews we schedule for tomorrow."

As Jenna and Watson drove over the small bridge to town, she looked west and saw rain clouds crawling across The Hamptons sky.

"Good thing you're here so you can protect me. Looks like a summer rain is out there." Jenna rubbed Watson's head and laughed, knowing what a big wimp he was when it came to lightening and thunder. She

23

snuggled him into a small blanket, cracked the windows, and went inside to meet with the Doc, Lara and Johnson.

***

"We found a strange oval shaped bruise cut deep into his chest, and finally it looks as if he had been strangled before being stabbed in his throat. That's what caused all the bleeding. Whoever did this meant to be sure he was really dead. It was a very violent act," concluded Doc as he showed them the bruise and knife wound in the throat.

"Any idea what type of instrument was used to stab him?" asked Troy.

Jenna pointed to Yellen's throat: "Those black marks around his throat, they look like the same black nail polish as was painted on his thumb nails. Not sure what the hell that's supposed to mean."

"Correct about the polish. As to what it is, I have no idea at this point. I took some samples and I'm analyzing them," Lara told her.

"Okay, we'll check with both of you tomorrow," Johnson replied as he and Jenna walked out and over to the police headquarters.

"Let me take a quick check on Watson. He's in my jeep." Jenna hurried out. She saw it had already rained briefly, leaving a cloudless, summer, Hamptons sky. She gave Watson a couple of treats, took him for a short walk and went back to meet with Troy about setting up tomorrow's interviews.

They agreed that in the morning Troy would interview Dr. Christian Keller and Jenna would meet with Dr. Alana Keller. Sergeant Miller would contact Larson's attorney, having gotten his name earlier at the crime scene, and request that he and Larson arrive at the station in the early afternoon. After Larson, Troy would bring Nora to the police station.

Pieces of this puzzle were not only missing, they seemed to be intentionally left out for reasons unknown.

Jenna was sure of one thing: Everyone involved so far seemed to be lying.

***

Held at 3:15 P.M., the press conference was short and not so sweet. After hearing a statement read by Detective Troy Johnson, the media was left hungering for more.

"There is little information so far, except to tell you that we have a lot of evidence to analyze and hope to have more information the next couple of days," Troy began. "Doc Bishop is in process of examining the body and Lara Stern, the evidence. Yes, Andre Yellen was wearing a yellow wig and stuffed in a gown designed by him." (They didn't need to know about the black nail polish, not yet.) "Yes, he was strangled, then stabbed in the throat and left by the swimming pool in the back yard of movie mogul Kevin Larson. Sergeant Miller will provide you with official updates on the case. Thank you for being here." Detective Johnson turned around, walked quickly back to his office and away from any questions . . . for now.

***

Sergeant Stan Miller had been with the police force in the Hamptons for over twelve years, after serving as a beat policeman in New York City for seven. Sergeant Miller never wanted to be anything other than a policeman, so he felt lucky to be able to do the work he was doing. One could say he was a combination of street-smart and compassionate. Both traits were a result of his young life having been marred by tragedy.

CHAPTER 4

SERGEANT STAN MILLER

When he was eight years old, Stan saw his father murder his mother.

He hid with his six-year-old sister under the bed in his room, holding her while covering her mouth so she wouldn't cry or scream. They waited … and waited … until he heard the front door slam shut. His mother was moaning in the living room. Crawling out from under the bed, he saw his mother bleeding from a bullet that, he later was told, had nicked her heart.

At eight, having lived with an abusive father all his life, he knew to quickly call 9-1-1. His heart was pounding and his sister wouldn't let go of his hand, tears streaming down her face.

"My mother's been shot. I'm afraid she's going to die. Please help us."

He gave his name, his address, his age and begged for help as the person on the other end of the phone kept asking questions to keep him calm until the police arrived. He gave his father's name and told how his dad had just shot his mother.

It seemed like an eternity to the youngsters, hand in hand, alone and scared, while they waited for the police to come. In fact, it was not more than five minutes before Stan and his sister Caryn heard the police and ambulance sirens.

Much of the rest was a blur to this too-old, eight-year-old. Over and over, he asked, "Will my mother be okay? Will she be okay? Can we go with her?"

"Son, let the ambulance people do their job. They're going to take your mother to the hospital while you tell me what happened."

The policeman in charge took him and his sister outside away from the blood stained carpet. He sat down with Stan and held him close to comfort him and help him feel safe. A policewoman had rushed to the house and was holding Stan's sister on her lap.

With relief flooding through him, Stan told the policeman about the years of abuse. The boy was finally able to tell someone who listened and seemed to care.

"He came home with a gun today, and he said he was going to kill all of us. My mother shoved Caryn and me into the bedroom, and she whispered to me to lock the door and hide. I was going to climb out the window and go for help, but I didn't dare leave my sister alone. I know she would have left the bedroom to be with our mother. We hid under the bed as we heard our mother crying and screaming and then, two gunshots—I think—maybe more. When we were pretty sure he had left, we ran out. I saw my mother lying on the floor bleeding and, well, you know the rest, I called 9-1-1.

"You're a very brave young man," the policeman was now holding both of Stan's hands, talking to him with sincere compassion. 'What is your full name?'"

"Stan, Stanley Milkowitz. My mom calls me Stan. My sister is Caryn. She's six, and I'm eight. Please, can we go see my mother?"

"I don't know if we can do that yet, Stan. Do you have any aunts or uncles or grandparents, anyone who can help look after you and your sister? Anyone we should call and tell what has happened here today?"

Stan was telling his story to Jenna. It was one he had told almost no one, but time had healed a lot and he was glad to have her as his friend.

"I sat very quiet, my sister was, too. Then I began to cry and told him we had a grandmother who had always been nice to us. She's my mother's mother and lives kind of far away. We've gone to visit her a few times. She had begged my mother to leave our father, saying he was a very bad man for hurting all of us. But then my father would plead with Mom to come home, saying it would be different. It never was."

"Stan, do you know how we can reach your grandmother?" Even as he stood to walk back inside with the boy, the policeman kept holding his hand.

Once back inside the house, where crime scene tape was wrapped around the living room, the boy went to a small drawer in the kitchen that had a few old keys, a pair of scissors, a half pack of gum and a small red phonebook in the back under an old note pad.

"My mother kept this hidden, but one day she showed me where it was. She told me not to tell my father and that if I ever needed help, my grandmother's phone number is in it. She even showed me which page. Also there are numbers of a few friends and of a rabbi she used to know before she was married. I never met him."

After taking the phonebook that Stan had handed to him, the policeman bent down to Stan's height and asked him if it was okay to call his grandmother for him. "I'd like to see if she could come and be here with you and Caryn."

"Then the policeman went back outside with the phonebook. Caryn was still sitting on the lap of the policewoman who had given her some juice and a small stuffed blue dog to hold."

Stan told how he could hear the policeman talking to his grandmother, telling her what happened. "She'll be here late tonight, Stan, and I promised her we'll take good care of you and Caryn until she gets here."

After he had heard that their grandmother was coming for them, quiet tears ran down eight-year-old Stanley Milkowitz's face.

Years later, he told the whole story to Jenna and Troy, when they were out having a drink, part of a closing-a-case ritual they all had with a few others in the community. They had wondered why he decided to be a policeman.

Finishing his story, Stanley Milkowitz told them he had changed his name to Stan Miller. "My mother died a few days later from the gunshot wounds, I never wanted my name to ever again be connected to my father's. Thankfully, we learned he was sent to jail for life without parole."

Jenna could hardly move listening to the rest of Stan's story. As both a reporter and a private investigator, she was always stunned that people could be so cruel, especially to helpless children.

"For the next eleven years, Caryn and I lived with my grandmother in a wonderful house in upstate New York, right outside of Albany, where she had lived with my grandfather before he had passed away a long time ago. I went to college thanks to my grandmother and student loans. She wanted me to continue and maybe be a lawyer, but I already knew I wanted to be a policeman."

"Is your grandmother still alive?"

"She is, and she is still living in her home. My sister lives only a few blocks from her. After Caryn went to college, she married. She and her husband have a home and a ten-year-old daughter. They own a small business together. Caryn and Grandma became very close after my mother was murdered. All three of us did. Her daughter is named after our mother, Ellen; Ellie for short."

"How did you get to The Hamptons?" Jenna's curiosity now in full swing!

"At age twenty-four, I went to the police academy. After graduating, I spent eight years as a police officer on the streets of New York City. In fact, I was often called in to work on cases of child abuse because they knew I was good with kids. One day, I saw that The Hampton Police Department was searching for some new officers and here I am. I was ready for a change."

"Did you ever hear from the policeman who came to your house that day?"

"I did, Jenna, until he retired a few years ago moved to Florida. He sent me a holiday and birthday card every year and always with a note saying that he hoped I was doing well and to let him know what I'm doing. I always did, when I sent him a holiday card in return every year. He helped me see that there is good in people, that there is a way of existing in the world to help people, not hurt them. Oh yeah, besides, I also promised my grandmother I would be a GOOD man."

"Well you certainly are, and someday, a GOOD woman is going to grab you for a husband," Jenna hugged him.

Jenna understood now why he never married. She, too, had secrets that had held her back from getting married, secrets that had a long-time hold on her.

CHAPTER 5

DATE NIGHT

Jenna and Dave, plus Troy and Marianna, went out together once every couple of months for what they called, "Date Night."

This time, they were having dinner at the ever popular Steak and Lobster House to celebrate Troy and Marianna's fifteenth wedding anniversary.

Four good friends, a table by an open window, the sound of the surf rising up to them, the stars peeking out in the night sky and the mild temperature requiring no jackets completed the evening. It seemed perfect. It *was* perfect for *them*, a brief time away from the demands of their busy lives.

Life was hectic for all of them.

Marianna not only oversaw the chaos of four school-aged children, she was also a high-school substitute math teacher. Jenna once told her she thought she was braver than the rest of them. With dark skin, very long wavy, dark brown hair, even big dark brown eyes, about 5' 4" tall, Marianna had grown up in a big family in Mexico. She had helped take care of her younger siblings and knew how to manage the challenges—and, yes, the chaos. Jenna was pretty sure she herself could not. Well, actually she did not even want to consider it! Catching murderers was easier, she once told Troy.

As dessert arrived, the evening had begun to cool, and the front door to the restaurant banged opened as a couple came in. They were loud, sounding more than slightly drunk, and demanded a table by the window.

The owner firmly told them several times, "There are none. We would be happy to have you sit at the bar, or we can give you a table in the far corner." Of course, they could even leave.

Jenna looked up as the commotion got louder and the couple became more difficult. "Troy, I think you might want to look at this." She nodded her head at the scene going on at the front of the restaurant.

They both turned to look at the couple and stared. It was Kevin Larson and Dr. Alana Keller. Jenna recognized her from photos Patricia had e-mailed to her.

"Who is that?" asked Dave.

Marianna asked, "What is going on back there?" They had also both turned to see the commotion.

Troy answered with a tone of disgust while still looking toward them. "The guy is Kevin Larson. His house was where we found the dead body of Andre Yellen."

Jenna added, "The woman is Dr. Christian Keller's wife, Dr. Alana Keller. They were co-chairs of the event that auctioned the gown Yellen was found dead in. That was less than forty-eight hours ago. They're quite a pair."

Looking like an aging fashion model, Dr. Alana Keller was tall, probably all of a size 2, with her very short dark hair, fashionably cut. Maybe she *had been* a model in her younger days. *Now*, she's an anorexic looking dermatologist to the rich and famous!

Jenna thought her husband, Dr. Christian Keller, was by far better looking than his wife. He was about the same height as she, a full head of grey hair, slender, almost lean but not quite, and a fake smile that his cosmetic surgery patients loved. The couple was indeed involved in beauty in The Hamptons.

Jenna remarked, a little sarcastically, "They do a whole lot of boob jobs, nose jobs, sucking fat out of anywhere and everywhere on the body and injecting patients with Botox and other poisons. They a busy team earning a great deal of money off people who seem to be 'dying to be beautiful'."

It took a brief second before Larson realized that the police detective and private investigator who had been at the murder scene at his home yesterday were also in the restaurant and had witnessed his tirade.

They all heard him as he grabbed Alana's hand and whispered to the owner, "Never mind, we're leaving," as he pulled her out the door.

"Sweetheart," Marianna said to her husband, "I can tell you one thing, I'm pretty sure she was wearing an Andre Yellen dress. I saw it in a fashion magazine. Yeah, I know, I'm addicted to reading those magazines."

"Glamour and style are actually a big part of life, certainly in The Hamptons and in fact many other places," Dave was grinning as he had seen Jenna flipping through pages of a Paris fashion magazine one time.

"Hey, I don't have to speak fluent French to understand what these clothes are saying to me. Buy me, buy me," Jenna laughed.

He smiled, gave her a loving hug without commenting. "I just like to look at the beautiful clothes," she smiled back.

"Marianna," asked Jenna, "can you do me a favor and find the magazine you saw it in and give it to Troy to bring to me tomorrow?"

Troy leaned back in his chair and grinned, "Jenna, what are you thinking? I've seen that look. You have an idea brewing about these two and their connection to Yellen. And yes, I will bring you the magazine tomorrow! Now let's enjoy the rest of our evening ... including dessert, of course."

"Something isn't right about them together, and their rushing out of here after they saw us watching them make a scene. I'm really curious what the hell is going on with them," Jenna took a taste of her delicious strawberry cheesecake.

It was a summer Hamptons night when the sunset changed the sky from clear blue to shades of red and purple. When the sun finally laid down in the horizon, it was still clear enough to see across the Long Island Sound to Connecticut.

Quiet returned to the restaurant. Only soft jazz music competed with the waves coming gently ashore. This was the real beauty of life in The Hamptons.

As they got up to leave, Troy pushed his chair close to the table so Marianna could get by him, and leaned over, "Jenna, let's you and I go visit those two together tomorrow instead of separately as we had planned. They looked at us like they wanted to murder us."

Neither of them realized that tomorrow was about to get even busier.

***

Next morning, at 6 A.M., Watson was barking like crazy. He heard someone banging on Jenna's door. Dave had spent the night and was on his way to see who it was, while at the same time Jenna's cell phone was ringing. As Dave opened the door to Troy, Jenna heard Troy on the phone. He was obviously determined to reach her at this early hour.

"Larson was found dead this morning. He was stuffed into an Andre Yellen gown."

Jenna quickly started to throw on jeans and a t-shirt while she shouted out to him, "When and where?"

"The station had a 9-1-1 call a half hour ago from a screaming Dr. Alana Keller. A security guard for the building where she has her practice out east saw her office door opened. He went in and found Larson's body dumped in the middle of her reception area. Dr. Keller called her husband, who told her to call our stations. The security guard had also notified his superior. I'm not sure who they called.

"I'm told he's wearing the gown with a note pinned to it that's says 'I'm a Yellen.' He's also wearing a blond wig and has black nail polish on his two thumb nails same as Yellen. Still don't know what the hell that all means, except we need to get out there—soon."

In less than ten minutes, Jenna was dressed, had grabbed her red leather jacket, and was ready to go out the door.

Dave told her, "Go! I'll lock up the house and take Watson with me for the day." He started to say, "I love you," and then thought better of it. Another time.

She gave him a kiss on the check and said to him, "I love you, thanks."

Dave grinned, waved goodbye, and went off to get Watson ready to spend the day playing with some of the other Irish setters at his place who were waiting to be adopted—and of course Aggie.

"I love her," he told Watson. Well, Watson knew that of course.

***

Getting into his police car to head out to the crime scene Troy told her, "I have someone at the station checking Larson's background and Doc is picking up Lara to meet us at Alana Keller's office. See if you can reach Patricia Tilton, maybe she can collect some background information for us as well."

"Patricia, it's Jenna and Detective Johnson, believe it or not, Kevin Larson was found dead this morning in Dr Alana Keller's office. Hope you can get out here before the story explodes. It's sure to be another media circus like Yellen's murder." Jenna was confident Patricia would bring some background information on Larson with her. They had discussed him at lunch yesterday in relation to Yellen's murder.

Then she put in a call to her parents. "Hi loved ones, need to talk to you, ask you what you might know about Fashion Queen Andre Yellen, movie mogul Kevin Larson, or cosmetic surgeon Dr. Christian Keller, and his wife, Dr. Alana Keller. By the way, Yellen and Larson have both been murdered out here. I promise I'm fine. So are Watson and Aggie, they're with Dave." She knew to reassure them or they would have the armed militia out here.

"Have you ever met any of them? Troy and I are on our way to where they found Larson's body. Let me know when you have a little free time to talk." After Jenna left the message, she then tried to concentrate on the ride Out East since traffic could be a problem almost any type of day "in season." But she kept wondering what could have happened after Larson and Alana's bad behavior at the restaurant last night and before he was found dead in her office this morning.

* * *

The scene of Larson's death had the same bizarre look and feel as Yellen's.

The security guard promised he hadn't touched anything as Jenna handed him her card and Detective Johnson went inside ahead of her.

Jenna told him, "Don't let anyone in from the media except Patricia Tilton. She's from the daily paper and I invited her to meet us here. I'm sure she will be quite vocal letting you know who she is. The rest of the media will soon be banging on the doors to get in for news and photos. Do not let any of them in."

Like Yellen, Larson was lying in a pool of blood, stabbed in the throat, and strangled, wearing a deep green Yellen gown. There was a note on the gown that said, "I'm a Yellen." As the guard reported, he was wearing a blond wig and his thumb nails were painted with black nail polish.

Doc and Lara arrived minutes behind Troy and Jenna. Lara immediately put on latex gloves and handed a pair to both Jenna and Troy. Meanwhile, Doc and his newest intern brought in the gurney to take Larson out to the medical van. Sergeant Miller was putting up crime scene tape and helping the guard keep the media out.

Doc quickly knelt at the body, commenting, "This certainly does appear to be the work of the same killer. Someone apparently had something against both of them. He has the same type of stab wounds in his throat as Yellen had."

"How long has he been dead?" asked Troy, bending over the body, pulling the ridiculous-looking blond wig off the corpse's head.

"Probably just a few hours. Only partial *rigor mortis* has set in and there doesn't seem to be any defensive wounds. They came up behind him, apparently before he had a chance to react. Detective, let's get him out of here. We'll get right on the autopsy."

Lara began looking around the room for evidence, bagging some fibers and a blood sample. After the body was removed, she found near the body a bottle of black nail polish that must have been dropped there by accident.

Showing it to Jenna before putting it in an evidence bag, "Can you tell what store it might have come from? There's no label on it. Possibly, it's been special ordered online?"

"I've never seen this type of polish," responded Jenna, showing it to Troy. "You're probably right about it being special ordered. Can you test it at the lab and check out what make it might be? It's actually thicker than regular polish and can probably be used for something else other than painting finger nails."

"Like what?" asked Troy.

"Touching up scratches or marks on ebony wood furniture or on a black car," answered Lara. "It's that thick."

Troy took a look at it and handed it back to Lara. All of them were wearing gloves at the crime scene, so they did not contaminate any evidence.

"This is getting weirder and weirder," said Doc, "with the strange polish, the Yellen gown, wherever that came from, and that cheap blond wig. Whoever did this sure has a perverted sense of justice, if that's what they think they're doing with these murders."

"Doc, Jenna and I will meet you at the morgue around 3 P.M. That should give you and Lara time to check out the body and the forensics."

Troy turned to Jenna. "The Kellers as well as Nora need to be brought to the station tomorrow. I'll have Sergeant Miller arrange meetings for us starting around 10 A.M. to give us time to review the reports from Doc and Lara and do some background checks on these other characters who seem connected to this case. And I sure as hell want to know about Nora Flynn's boyfriend and her brother! Who are they, and where are they?"

Jenna agreed, but something was else was bothering her. "Troy, let's start with Alana Keller. We need to know where she and Larson went after they left the restaurant last night. What exactly was their relationship? Where was she when Larson was killed? And how did he get into her office?"

"Jenna, yeah, I know, we have a lot more questions then answers at this point."

"What do we have here now?" Patricia Tilton had just walked inside, got an update from Jenna, and looked around at the bizarre crime scene. "Who found him here?"

"The night security guard. He's the one I told to let you inside when you got here. Let's go ask him a few questions, maybe he knows if there's a tape of people entering the building. I'll tell Troy to meet us outside."

***

It was almost nine-thirty in the morning by the time Troy and Jenna stopped for coffee and a sweet roll. Neither of them had time for coffee before getting to the murder scene. Jenna also picked up several of the free weekly magazines, known as the local rags. Each week there were many pages of photos from parties to fundraising events. Several of them had photos of one or more of the Kellers, Larson and Yellen.

"Larson and Yellen appear very much like a couple." Jenna was poking at Troy getting him to look at the photos. "Troy, check these out, they're almost racy. Both of them are naked to the waist! In this one, Yellen is hugging Larson. Well, maybe they're not racy for The Hamptons."

"Certainly seems like they were much more than just friends," Troy responded, pointing to several other photos. It also reminded him that he had the magazine Marianna had given him.

Looking through that later would give them even more questions.

***

On the way back to the station, Troy told Jenna, "I had Sergeant Miller take the security camera from the lobby of the building. Maybe it will show who might have come in and out during the night or if there were any witnesses. He's going to see if someone at the station can help us with that."

While Troy was talking, Jenna's phone beeped, but she waited for whomever it was to leave a message.

In any investigation, clues, contacts or witnesses could show up when you least expected it.

CHAPTER 6

WITNESS

"Ma'am," said the voice on the message, "my name is James Parker. I'm the security guard for the building where the man was found dead this morning. You gave me your card when you came in. I believe I might have something interesting for you. Not sure."

Jenna called James Parker right back. She was still very curious why he had left in what seemed like a big hurry.

"James, I'll meet you at eleven-thirty. There's a coffee shop on Main Street in the middle of town near the police station. If you have a problem with that, my cell number is on the card you have"

Waiting at a corner table, she recognized him, even without his security guard uniform. James was truly good looking, probably in his late thirties or early forties, light brown hair, great cheekbones and a dimple in his chin. When she got closer, she thought he had some of the saddest brown eyes she had ever seen.

As he seemed to struggle to get up, she reached out to shake his hand. "Please, James, call me Jenna."

She sensed he was nervous, uncomfortable. He had something to tell her and seemed unsure of himself. His laptop computer was on the table next to a cup of coffee he had barely touched.

"So, how long have you been a security guard at that building?"

"Only about five months."

"Did you ever meet Dr. Alana Keller?"

For some reason, Jenna instinctively felt she needed to take this slow and allow him time to find it easy to talk to her "I was curious why you left before Detective Johnson or I had a chance to talk to you. I was going to call the security company to get your name and a way to reach you. You're not in trouble. I just wondered if you saw anything about the murder that might be useful to the investigation."

"I got scared. I'm sorry. My shift was actually over, so I left," James looked at her with those sad eyes that touched Jenna deeply.

"I can't afford to lose my job, so can what I want to show you be confidential, at least until you see what it is? I mean, I know if it's really serious evidence you'll have to use it."

"Of course, for now this is between you and me."

Jenna watched him open his computer—click, click, click—with ease and great expertise that was really impressive. Then he turned the computer around to show her something happening on the screen.

James began, "Before you look at this, my reason for being so hesitant is because I had switched on my computer, which was running a special program. I'm not supposed to have it on. When I heard a terrible noise and commotion in the building, I rushed to see what was happening, and I forgot to turn it off. By the time I got to Dr. Keller's office, whoever had been there was gone. The body was on her floor stuffed into a dress and a blond wig."

"Why didn't you call 9-1-1?"

"I immediately called the office of the company that hired me. Then I called the doctor, whose number I had been given in case of an emergency. When I was hired, I was told if they think it's a big problem, they'll call 9-1-1, so there's no false alarms going to the police."

"What does your computer have to do with this?" Jenna sat up, bending over to look at the screen.

"Look. Here!"

"James, who is that person on the screen? He or she seems to be running with his back to it."

"Ma'am—sorry, Jenna—I don't know who it is. I began to think it could be the person who left the body in Dr. Keller's office. The computer is time stamped exactly when all the noise happened. I've been developing a program I can use for a security business idea I have. The time shows someone arriving at 2:45 A.M. and leaving at 3 A.M."

"Has anyone else seen this information?"

"No. I left with my computer and wasn't sure what to do. Then I looked at your card, saw you're a private investigator and knew you would know what I should do."

"James, is there any way to identify who the person is?"

"Not exactly. If I had access to more sophisticated equipment, we could most likely identify at least if it's a man or woman, their height, body build, and even the shape of the head and the color of their hair."

"Okay. Lara Stern is the head of the forensic crime lab for the East End of Long Island. She probably has equipment that can do that. I realize you're concerned about your job, and I promise we can keep this quiet, at least for now. This is extremely helpful and important, James."

"Yeah. Guess I kinda figured that."

"Can we take it over to the crime lab now? It's nearby. I'll call and tell her we're coming and that we need her help with what's on your computer." Jenna was already on the phone to the lab.

"Today is my day off. I guess so," James coughed nervously.

"Thanks for trusting me, James. Let's just see what happens."

James Parker closed his computer, put it in a dark tan backpack and got up to follow Jenna to the forensic lab. He limped as he got out from behind the table and looked at her, quietly telling her, "I'm a vet. I lost part of my leg during a tour in Afghanistan."

"Oh, James, I'm so sorry. Well, it looks to me like it didn't harm your brain any. Thank goodness. I have a feeling you're a computer whiz, and we sure could use some help in that area. We'll talk about that after we get this figured out."

Jenna knew she wanted to help James Parker. It was immediate, instinctive. She knew that there was probably a place for him where his life and service really could matter and maybe make his sad eyes perhaps a little less sad. There was something about James. She liked him. It was that simple.

It was after noon when they got to the lab. Lara was waiting for them, curious what this was all about.

"Lara Stern, James Parker. Lara, I asked James to show you something he picked up on his computer at the crime scene this morning. He was the night security guard there and had called in the murder."

Once again he clicked onto the screen showing the person entering and leaving the building and at what times. James pointed to the person, wanting to know if Lara could enhance the image in a way to show more about that person. It might not show the whole face, but at least it might get a better image of the possible culprit.

"See, he or she probably figured there were some security cameras so the face is hidden. But I've been developing a new recognition program for a business I'm hoping to start, so I was able to pick up more nuances than a typical security camera might."

"No kidding," said Lara looking closer. "Let's see how it functions and interacts with my equipment."

Jenna stood back and watched. Lara and James were in their own world of computer genius that she found remarkable. Within minutes, they had begun working together as if they had worked together like this for years.

"Jenna, we got something," Lara called her over to show her what they had done.

"Okay, we need to call Troy and Doc so they can see this. James, I promise we'll make things all right for you. Please trust us."

***

Within fifteen minutes Troy, Jenna and Lara were looking at the images James had captured on his computer. They were now blown up and in a format that helped them to identify several key traits of the person going in and out. Doc came in only briefly since he was still doing the autopsy of Kevin Larson.

"Definitely a man, looks about 5'9', dark hair, wearing a dark, solid grey top of some sort. He has something wrong with his back, he's bent over slightly." Troy was pointing all this out as Lara and James went back to try to highlight the man's face, even though it only showed a little bit of the side of it.

"We have all we can get from this for now." Lara turned to look at Troy and Jenna, "If it's okay with you guys, I'd like James to work more on this with me for the next couple of hours. In fact, I'll order in some lunch for us." Lara immediately pulled out some lunch menus and passed them over to James.

Jenna and Troy just looked at each other, smiling, knowing. Something surely was happening between those two.

***

"We need to help him. He told me he lost part of his leg in Afghanistan, and his eyes were so sad when we met. Of course, they sure didn't look that sad when he was working with Lara just now," Jenna commented as she and Troy went out for pizza and, of course, to discuss the case. She also ordered a diet soda, knowing that soda was really bad for her and not giving a damn, not after two murders.

"I saw he was limping, wondered what it was," Troy commented, then ordered a beer and house special pizza for both of them.

"Do you think he has PTSD?" asked Jenna.

"I guess it's possible. Experiencing or witnessing a horrible or tragic event can cause PTSD. The horrors of war sure fit that definition."

"Also like losing his leg?"

"Sure, Jenna, for James losing part of a leg in a war, and probably even some friends had to be awful for him. PTSD can last for years."

"What do you think of James and Lara? Seems they fell in sudden like with each other!"

At that moment, Jenna got a call. "Jenna, it's James and Lara. We think we found something that could be really helpful. Lara's putting it up on her equipment. We can see the knife he had with him—and it is a he."

"Great, Detective Johnson and I will be there shortly."

"By the way—the knife is in his left hand."

***

Jenna also had a message from her mother. "Yes, we've met both victims as well as the Kellers."

43

CHAPTER 7

THE PRESTONS

The Prestons, Jenna's parents, were extremely wealthy. They were well connected to many people in Manhattan society circles, the Los Angeles movie industry, as well as local and national political candidates they supported. Her father, Mathew Preston, a corporate attorney, had an impressive list of clients. Over the past forty plus years, his firm, which was started before Jenna was born, had grown to have two-dozen partners, numerous associates and staff; with offices in Manhattan, Washington, D.C., and Los Angeles.

It was Jenna's mother who called her back first. Jenna and her mother had a loving relationship. Her mother was down to earth despite living a life of privilege, and she was always easy to talk to and generous in many ways. An only child, Jenna Preston was raised in a life of privilege—private schools, trips abroad, money for pretty clothes and more. Grace Preston had doted on her, but once told her, quite firmly, "Darling, you might be spoiled, but your father and I refuse to let you become a spoiled brat."

Now in her sixties, still slender, the same height and blue eyes as Jenna, with short hair more gray than not, Grace Preston was one of those women who would probably still be attractive when she was in her nineties.

Smiling at thoughts of her mother, Jenna answered the phone to hear her mother say, "Hello dear, those are some charming characters you asked your father and me about."

"I thought you might have met or known some or a few of them over the years."

"Know them, yes. Socialize, no. They have been at various events we've attended. Your father and I found the Kellers particularly arrogant. They were often heard saying crude remarks that they thought were funny. They wanted attention and to have others treat them as if they were very important. We did our best to avoid them."

"Did you ever see Andre Yellen or Kevin Larson together, especially looking like they were a couple?"

"Mom?" Her mother had been quiet for a long moment it seemed.

"Sorry, I was trying to recall when we saw them last and how they were together. Yes, in the last few years, they began to show up together. They were not flaunting a relationship, but it was fairly obvious there was one. I recall remarking to your father that they made a rather interesting couple, both of them quite successful in their careers."

"Interesting couple... I would say so," mused Jenna. "Even more interesting is that both of them have been murdered out here within days of each other and in a similar fashion."

"Well, it's in the papers and on the news here. Nothing seems to get past the twenty-four hour news cycle anymore. There have been all sorts of seedy suggestions about them. News people went on and on about their world of excessive beauty and beautiful people, how they had been killed, and of course the big question—who murdered them?"

"We are certainly working on that. Troy and I have some people we're getting ready to interview tomorrow, including both Dr. Kellers."

"Jenna, do you really think it's possible that one of them did this?"

"Mom, anything is possible with such arrogant, self-centered people. Did you ever see Larson and Yellen, talking or sitting with the Kellers?"

"Maybe a couple of times. People table-hop so much at these events. That's all I know dear, except for a whole lot of gossip that is the same gossip you find on the TV and Page Six in the New York paper. Do you still want your father to call you? He most likely knows more about them than I do, perhaps through some business affairs."

"I would, Mom. Ask Dad to call me on my cell phone when he has time. I'd like to find out what he might know about them and if he ever met with any of them outside of these events you've seen them at."

Having promised she would have him call, before hanging up, Grace Preston told her daughter, her only child, "I'll have him call you ... Jenna please be careful. You know we love you very much, my dear."

"Love you lots, too. Dave and I plan a visit soon, and maybe we can even introduce you to Aggie."

They both laughed.

***

Mathew Preston soon called. "Jenna, hi honey. It's Dad." She truly adored, as well as admired him.

"Hi, Dad. You most likely heard or read that both Andre Yellen and Kevin Larson have been murdered only a day apart. Dr. Alana and Dr. Christian Keller seem to be involved somehow, although I'm not sure how yet. When I spoke to Mom earlier she said you and she had seen them at various events in the city."

"Well," he began. She remembered as an attorney he would be very thoughtful of what he was saying, even to Jenna. "Yes, we did. Larson and Yellen were often together, having been romantically involved for quite a few years," he told her.

She asked, "Did you know either of then personally or professionally?"

"About three years ago," he said, "they came to see me about writing their wills. Obviously I can't tell you any more than that."

"Of course," Jenna replied. "Did you see them out together at any recent events?"

"In fact, we did. The last event when we saw them must have been the end of April. I thought it was strange how they seemed to be ignoring each other. A little later, I saw them having a screaming match with the two doctors you mentioned."

"Do you know those doctors?"

"Barely," replied her Dad. "From the first time I met them four or five years ago, I found them rather obnoxious, and your mother and I avoided them as much as possible."

"My sentiments exactly," Jenna said.

"If I think of anything else I'll call you back," he told her.

They said goodbyes and I love you, after her father reminded her of how dangerous the situation seemed.

She had a feeling it was about to get a whole lot more dangerous now.

***

Twenty-minutes after their conversation ended, Mathew Preston called his daughter again. "Jenna, I realized I saw Dr. Christian Keller at a ball game a few weeks ago. He was there with a couple of burly looking guys with very big muscles. They looked like they were threatening him. That made me recall that there had been some stories about his betting and heavy losses."

"Did he know you saw him?"

"No, I don't think so. I turned around and walked away from where they were going at it."

"You're the best, thanks."

"No thanks necessary, just plan on going to a ball game with me later this month."

Mathew Preston loved baseball.

He had started taking Jenna to ballgames when she was only five years old, always sitting behind home plate or third base.

"I would love to," Jenna said as she hung up, thinking … wait until Troy hears about this!

THE DOCTORS KELLER

Sergeant Stan Miller called Dr. Alana Keller to be at the station, the next day, Wednesday, 10 A.M. He then called Dr. Christian Keller to be at the station at 11:00 A.M. "Be prompt," he told them.

Then he called Nora Flynn.

"I'm Sergeant Miller. Detective Johnson said I'm to pick you up for a noon meeting at the station with him and Jenna Preston. Be sure you're ready."

Naturally, both of the Kellers' attorneys called, demanding to know why their clients had been called to the station for an interview. It was common knowledge they were getting a divorce. Both of them were already seeing other people.

"Because this is a very serious murder case, and if you don't show up Detective Johnson said he'll issue an arrest warrant for your client!" He gave the same message to both attorneys.

"Of course I'll be there with my client. I was asking what this was about. That can't be too difficult for you to answer!" That snippy remark coming from Christian's attorney.

Click. Sargent Miller hung up on him.

***

The next morning Dr. Alana Keller was in and out of the interview and the police station in less than twenty minutes. She was wearing black slacks and a grey silk blouse and three inch steel grey heels, makeup and hair perfect. Speaking for her, the New York lawyer said she was in shock from the incident and asked if it were possible for them to speak with her tomorrow.

"Some incident, excuse me," Detective Johnson stood up and threw photos of the two dead men across the table as Alana Keller and her attorney got up to leave. "This was not an *incident*. It was *murder*, and I assure you that Dr. Keller will need to speak with us soon or we will arrest her for withholding evidence in a murder investigation."

Jenna had watched her closely as the detective asked three questions: "Where did you and Larson go after you left the restaurant last night? What exactly was your relationship with him? How could someone get into your office and leave his body there?"

Jenna showed she was also clearly furious at their insensitivity to two men being murdered by tossing *more* photos of both dead men at Alana.

"It's known you have slept with these two men. Detective Johnson and I saw you with Kevin Larson last night, hours before he was killed. Where did you go last night after you left the restaurant?" demanded Jenna.

"I went home. He was acting obnoxious. I had my own car and left him in the parking lot. I don't know who killed him. I know I didn't," Alana Keller yelled.

Her attorney finally took her by the arm, "Let's go. They have no reason to hold you here."

As the two were leaving, Detective Johnson warned them to be available again within the next twenty-four hours.

***

Dr. Christian Keller was another matter all together. Although he, too, had his attorney with him, he refused to shut him up.

Keller was dressed as if he was off to the country club for drinks in his white linen pants, navy silk polo shirt and expensive loafers. Hampton chic meant no socks, of course.

"Do you have any knowledge of these two murders? Do you know who might have committed them?" Again Detective Johnson shoved photos of the two murdered men in front of the suspect.

Christian Keller's attorney looked like he just got off the Hampton Jitney for a weekend of tennis and partying. The very popular Hampton Jitney was a luxury bus service that took people back and forth from the city to various destinations in The Hamptons and the East End. It was 'in' to say "I'll take the Jitney to The Hamptons."

During the summer season, the schedule increased significantly. Along with that came a whole lot of egos and crazies, who fought for front seats, used cell phones when not allowed and claimed they had reservations when they clearly had not made them.

The Hampton Jitney was a happening and the whole scene got crazier and crazier each year.

Dr. Christian Keller's attorney was over six-feet with dark hair slicked back. He was also dressed in white slacks and a white polo shirt, with loafers and, again, no socks. Keller had apparently paid his attorney with some serious plastic surgery. Although a man in his fifties, he had no wrinkles, a perfect nose and a very flat belly. Liposuction could do that.

Cool and aloof, the attorney kept instructing Dr. Keller, "Christian, do not answer any questions." However, the ego driven, blow-hard doctor continued to act like a jerk, declaring, "I don't know a damn thing about these murders."

Jenna and Troy didn't believe him for a minute.

"Why don't you ask my wife? I understand Larson's body was found in her office. Surely you know they've been seen around town recently." He almost drooled when he said it.

Jenna looked at Keller as if he had just landed on earth. "Didn't that bother you? Weren't you the least bit concerned about your professional reputations?"

"Oh, please! Our friends know we're living apart and are ready to separate— permanently. Alana and I agreed to stay together over the summer for business reasons only. Our medical practices are quite lucrative, and we provide many referrals to each other. So you see, in truth, I don't give a damn what she does or who she does it with, since we are parting ways. Very soon after this! That's for sure," declared Dr. Keller.

His attorney sat back and let the man act the fool he apparently was.

Detective Johnson, staring at Keller, demanded to know, "Where were you last night between 1 and 5 P.M.?"

"Home."

"Do you have any witnesses?"

"Sure, my pain-in-the-ass wife!"

"Why were you so angry about Yellen's gown being donated for the fundraiser?"

At that, Keller's attorney stood up and said, "No comment." He literally grabbed the good doctor by the arm, pulling him up from the chair while telling Detective Johnson and Jenna, "You want any more answers? Subpoena him."

"What is your relationship with Nora Flynn?"

Keller didn't answer. He flinched, but only for a second. It was a second too long for Jenna.

As they walked out of the room, Detective Johnson told Dr. Keller the same thing he told his wife and her attorney: "We expect we'll want you back here within twenty-four hours."

"That was it," said Jenna after they left.

"What do you mean, that was it?" Troy looked at her as if she was crazy. They were headed to the coroner's lab where Doc and Lara would probably still be sorting through evidence.

"His body language. It changed. He kept rubbing his hands and blinking a lot. That question you threw at him about Nora almost stopped him in his tracks as they were walking out of here. There's got to be more to his relationship with her."

"Think they were having an affair?" Troy asked.

"Maybe," answered Jenna.

"Maybe?" Troy turned and stopped in front of her. "What more?"

Jenna reminded Troy, "I thought she mentioned she had a boyfriend and a brother who live near by somewhere. And it seems one or the other often stays with her. Neither of them works much and both often need money from her. They seem to have been a couple of freeloaders, and she's probably put up with it for a long time."

"Yeah, well, where are they? We need to talk to both of them as soon as possible."

***

Sergeant Miller brought Nora into Detective Johnson's office, not wanting to freak her out too much by an interrogation room. As Miller left they could hear him on his phone, "Sir, I'm sorry, you can yell at me all you want. There is nothing new to tell about the Yellen and Larson murders. That's what you will have to tell your radio news program listeners."

Click went the phone.

"We better come up with something to give the media or they'll keep hounding Miller."

"Better him than me," laughed Troy.

CHAPTER 8

NORA

Jenna went to see Lara, while Troy went to talk to Doc, "Troy, so far we don't have any forensic evidence linking Nora or the doctors to the murders. Lara said we should check with her later this afternoon."

On the way to the interrogation room, they agreed they needed to know:

What type of instrument killed Yellen and Larson?

What made that deep mark on Yellen's chest?

Why that black nail polish?

Whose DNA was on the pool wall?

Almost everyone seems to be either lying or withholding information.

***

"Andre Yellen is dead! Kevin Larson is dead! Nora, you told us you knew Andre Yellen." Detective Johnson stood across from Nora Flynn staring at her, almost shouting.

Nora nodded, "Yes," as if talking would make her break in pieces.

"Did you ever meet Kevin Larson?"

Again, nodding, this time, "No."

"Are you afraid of Dr. Christian Keller?" asked Jenna.

"You told us he threatened you after you had been handed the gown the other evening," added Detective Johnson.

Nora turned to look at the door where she came in, as if she was looking to escape. Right behind her there was a one-way mirror that did not allow her to see out into the corridor.

As Nora Flynn had been coming into the interrogation room, Dr. Christian Keller was leaving. Neither of them said anything to each other. Their intentionally ignoring each other seemed way too obvious to Jenna.

"Nora, something isn't right with your explanation about the fundraising event and that gown."

"I want to leave. Please, just let me go. I'll be fine," cried Nora. "Dr. Keller, my boss, was upset the other night, but I'm sure he'll even let me keep my job."

As Detective Johnson and Jenna were about to continue the interview, Nora suddenly stopped, looked calmly at them. "A friend of mine said I should ask you if I need an attorney."

Jenna and Troy nodded to each other, stood up, Troy walking out first. He looked back at Nora, told her with a disgusted tone in his voice, "You can leave now."

Jenna wanted something more. "Nora before you leave, I want the names of your boyfriend and your brother. And, how can we reach them."

Nora looked surprised at the question. "Why?"

"Because we think it's important, that's why."

"My boyfriend is Tom Overton. He lives in a small apartment on the North Fork, and I haven't seen or heard from him in a couple days. In fact, he hasn't even answered any of my calls. As for my brother, Patrick Flynn, he could be anywhere. Some of the time he stays with me. Neither of them have full-time jobs, and I don't know what they might be up to."

"Nora, do your brother and boyfriend know each other?"

"Sure, sometimes they both stay overnight at my place."

"Have they been there recently?"

"A couple times in the past few weeks. Please let me leave now," Nora was nearly in a state of panic from what Jenna could see. She was pacing back and forth. Her face was all flushed, and she had tears in her eyes.

"Again with the tears," thought Jenna. "Nora, don't leave the area, we're going to want to talk to you again and most likely soon." Jenna knew Troy wasn't anywhere near done with her, only done for now.

Neither Jenna nor Troy had responded to her regarding an attorney. They let the question and her concern hang in mid-air.

As Nora was about to walk out the door of the police station, Jenna casually asked, "By the way, is your brother or boyfriend left handed?"

"Both of them."

***

Sergeant Miller had retrieved the police records of Tom Overton and Patrick Flynn and brought them to Detective Johnson. Both of them had plenty of trouble with the law in the past.

It turned out Overton had lived off and on, and off and on, again, with Nora. Over the years he had half a dozen different jobs, from parking cars to being a waiter at a couple of different restaurants. He wasn't very good at any of them and was fired after a few months. Overton was always looking for ways to make money by hustling or scheming, mostly without doing much work. Her brother wasn't much better.

"I get lonely, so I let him them stay with me when they want," Nora later told Jenna.

***

As soon as Nora got home, she made a call. Her hands were shaking and she paced back and forth, sounding every bit as panicked as she was and asked, "Can we get together? I'm scared. The police asked me a lot of questions this afternoon. They picked me up and took me there. I think they're going to figure out what really happened. I asked them if I needed an attorney so they let me go. And, they told me they're going to want to talk to me again—soon!"

"I'll be over later tonight." Click went the phone on the other end.

Nora knew she wasn't very smart, especially when it came to men, but she had been around enough to know something wasn't right.

Her experience with losers caused her to rethink that call. She waited about fifteen minutes, called back and told him, "You better not come by tonight. The police or that private investigator might be having me watched."

Then she called her best friend, Cate Ashton, who worked as a nurse's aide at a local hospital. "Can I spend the night at your place? I'll tell you all about what's happening when I see you."

"Of course," Cate replied, "come by after 5 P.M. I'll bring dinner home for us."

Nora considered that maybe she was overly concerned. Still, she felt better knowing she would be staying away from her house tonight. She decided that when she talked to Cate later, she was going to record the whole story ... just in case.

She packed an overnight bag, grabbed her old fashioned tape recorder, a couple of tapes and stopped at the drugstore for new batteries.

Yet, it wasn't really clear what "just in case" might be!

***

The next morning, Jenna left Troy a message. "I'm on my way to Nora's house, can you meet me there? She stayed overnight with a friend, stopped home this morning before going to work and found her place had been ransacked. There was a message on her wall, 'you could be next.' It was written in black nail polish."

Jenna continued: "I've been out East, doing some work for Kristin Sterling's firm, checking out recent plover killings. I'll fill you in on that later. I'll be at Nora's in about a half hour. I thought it was strange that she wasn't crying. She sounded damn angry. I'll play the message for you later."

"Jenna, I'll be there soon, and I'll ask Lara to go over there as soon as possible." Troy was in the Coroner's lab in an early morning meeting with Doc and Lara, the three of them going over evidence of the two murder cases.

"So far," Troy began, "we know they were both first strangled, then stabbed with some type of knife, by apparently someone who is left handed, and for some yet unexplained reason, each of them was stuffed in a Yellen gown wearing a cheap blond wig and strange black nail polish on their thumbnails."

Doc showed him an x-ray pointed to the chest area. "Yellen also had that wound with some kind of crystals in it. Larson didn't have that."

"Lara, did you figure out what those crystals are yet?" Troy stared closely at the x-ray, curious. "Do you think they could have rubbed off something someone was wearing?"

Lara gathered up her evidence case, getting ready to head back to Nora's to check on what might have been left as a result of her latest drama. "Possible. Hard to tell at this point. I'm waiting for some test results. Should have them back later in the day."

Meantime, in the car going to Nora's, Jenna replayed the message, having left the plovers to their own plight for now.

"Jenna, this is Nora Flynn, my place has been ransacked. The S.O.B. left a message for me on my wall that I could be next. Can you get here soon? I need to tell you and Detective Johnson the whole story about this mess. Fortunately, I stayed at a friend's house last night."

"I'll be there in a half hour. Detective Johnson should be there sooner. Lock up your house and wait for us."

"Okay. I'm still trying to find my boyfriend or my brother."

With them out of touch or even missing, Nora sensed she had an even bigger problem that involved her boyfriend and her brother.

***

Tom Overton was nowhere to be found. Neither was Patrick Flynn.

Nora left a message for Tom at his apartment, a crummy studio behind another house. Then she called a couple of the bars Tom frequented and a gas station a buddy of his owned where he would hang out drinking beer when he wasn't working. Which was way too often.

It was harder to know where her brother might be. Probably at one of the many hookers he kept company with. She often thought it possible that he could be their pimp. He was usually broke, borrowing money from her that, of course, he never paid back.

Leaving more messages, she paced back and forth, and kept checking that the doors were locked. "Tom, something bad happened.

If you get my message, please come over and stay with me. I'm waiting for the police to get here, and I am scared as hell."

Tom never got back to her.

She left the same message for Patrick. He also never got back to her.

"Where the hell are you two?" Nora screamed to the mess in her home that felt even smaller and more depressing than usual.

One bar owner she spoke to complained, "Hey, we haven't seen Tom in a couple days. He still owes me for a few beers. You might like to know he was with your brother. They kept laughing about how thanks to you they were going to be in the dough! Oh yeah, they even talked about going away from here, maybe somewhere out of the country. They kept bragging they were going to have a life of 'broads and booze,' and they couldn't wait to get out of this lousy place. Mostly I ignored them. They were both drunk, as usual. They became so loud and obnoxious that we practically threw them out."

"What is that all about?" Nora wondered.

Nora sat on her cheap sofa, old and stained, with the black nail polish threat written on the wall behind her and started to cry again. This time, she was pretty sure she was in big trouble.

Probably, and so were Tom and Patrick!

CHAPTER 9

A FEW MORE
MURDERS

In the middle of the high-profile murder investigation, which was complicated by the irrational way the bodies had been dressed, Kristin left Jenna a message.

"Jenna, please call me. It's important. I know you're busy with the recent 'fashion' murders out here, but if possible I desperately need you to do an investigation at the East Hampton beach. Five plovers have been killed!"

In the very early morning of the next day, Jenna was out East checking the plover's nesting area. It was hard to say no to Kristin. Since Jenna had gotten her license, and even back when she was still an investigative reporter, Kristin had been giving Jenna investigative work for the Environmental Law Firm. A drama played out yearly between the nesting rights for piping plovers and Hampton homeowners. A significant number of the latter were usually very annoyed over beach restrictions because of the endangered birds. Jenna was well aware of the history of these little fuzzy birds. She had written about them when she was working as a reporter for the local paper.

It was an extremely controversial issue, with environmentalists, as well as nature and bird lovers, versus those who found the restrictions unfair to people who have spent thousands to be in The Hamptons.

"Piping Plovers are an endangered species of small birds who each spring and summer nest, amongst other places, on the East Hampton beach. They are protected by law, but of course, crows, foxes and feral cats don't know that. Human predators are a supposed to follow the law."

Kristin told her, "Five of the plovers were found dead yesterday afternoon, apparently having been run over by some vehicle. It could have been a motorcycle, a small car or even a bicycle. We aren't sure. We think it's possible they were killed first by some kind of pellet gun, according to the people who found them and reported it to the police and also to us."

"Email me directions where exactly the site is located. I'll get out there early before traffic starts to build up." Jenna sat back, let out a sigh and pondered aloud, "Great, more murders."

***

The top ten list of things hated in The Hamptons in summer began with traffic congestion. Running a pretty close second were the haters and harassers of the plovers. (True, they did take over a good piece of prime beach.)

Local media had their own fights over them. Editorials ranged from those who wanted to get rid of the plovers all together to those who sided with the environmentalists intent on protecting the birds.

It was the same every summer, and each year it seemed to get nastier and nastier. Now someone had gone to the extreme and actually killed some of those fuzzy little plovers.

***

The scene on the beach reminded Jenna of something familiar, something maybe that she heard during the very recent Yellen and Larson murder investigations. She wasn't at all sure what.

The tire tracks appeared in the plover nesting area. She wasn't sure what type of vehicle made them. She took photos of the area and the tire tracks and decided she would come back again tomorrow.

Jenna called Kristin: "I'm leaving the plover nesting area now. However, I plan to come back tomorrow and attach a tiny camera to one of the fence poles. Meantime, I'll also see if I can match up tires from photos I just took."

Getting into her jeep, she looked out at the ocean with the surf flowing out and then back, touching the sand and back out again. She thought about how much she loved this piece of nature. But today felt different.

Too many murders!

For some reason, all that was happening reminded Jenna of her grandmother and the secret her grandmother told her when she was a teenager. Why was she thinking of all this now? "Maybe it's about being violated," Jenna said aloud.

The memory of advice from her grandmother that she should always protect herself almost felt like a warning of danger, as if there was a threat to her way of life or perhaps—to her very life.

Jenna felt as if the secret were taking its toll on her heart and soul, *after this case, I think it's time to face my own demons.*

Staring at the motion of the ocean waves from inside her car, Jenna called Kristin again. "I'm going to call the local police to check if there have been any complaints or arrests out East for drunken behavior in the past couple weeks."

Later Jenna got her answer: "Yes."

This time Jenna left a message while at a standstill in Hampton traffic. "Kristin, I have some names of DWI arrests. I'll email them to you. Cars are moving, have to go."

Her cell phone rang, stopping all those unsettling thoughts. For now.

"Hi. Watson and Aggie want to be sure you're coming here for dinner later. We'll see you around six unless I hear otherwise from you. Oh, by the way, it's Dave."

Jenna knew he must have had a big smile as he made this call. He was quite the charmer.

CHAPTER 10

CONNECTING
THE CLUES

"It doesn't make any sense!" Troy was clearly frustrated.

"Jenna, so far the facts are these: deaths, denials, lies, suspects with high-profile lawyers, and a couple of guys missing who I think could be involved. We also have plenty of publicity photos of the murdered men showing all sorts of connections between them and the doctors."

"Hey, believe me Troy, I know all too well. Two high-profile men dead, two well-know doctors involved and lawyered up, a young woman telling lies, plus her boyfriend and her brother both MIA," said Jenna, "and of course I also have the case of the murdered plovers!"

Jenna was remembering a conversation with Kristin and Patricia after the last murder case was closed.

"Most murders are committed in the name of some misguided reason that was held in the murderer's mind," Kristin told them."

Jenna adding, "Right, the culprit believes they had been wronged or even betrayed in some way. Then, their anger causes them to seek out revenge, to behave in a vengeful and cruel manner."

Patricia was much more practical, " of course, he or she could simply be a psychopath. There is always that possibility."

"Always carry with you a way to get to the truth, from your head and your heart. Know who you can trust, and don't betray your own instincts," were Jenna's grandmother's words to her years ago.

"What was the truth here?" Jenna wondered. Neither Troy nor she had been able to get to it. Not yet.

***

"Watson, let's take a walk."

Jenna had stopped home for her notes and to get herself and Watson ready to go to Dave's. Not that there was a lot to do. She had kept some overnight and casual clothes at his place, as well as a supply of her beauty needs, such as a hairdryer. Hey, she thought smiling, "A girl needs to know her priorities."

First she decided she and Watson both needed to take a walk.

Watson was ready like a young lover. He and Jenna walked toward the beach near her home, she breathing in the amazing sea air, he wagging his tail and bouncing from tree to tree. She loved this dog! His energy and enthusiasm was such a delight to her. His playfulness kept her on her toes, especially if they met another dog when they were walking. Watson seemed to have quite an affinity for the females.

Out walking, Jenna became even more aware of how troubled she was by their interviews with Nora and both Doctor Kellers. The pieces absolutely did not fit!

"Hey Troy, I'm taking a walk with Watson. Want to meet us at our favorite bench? Bring coffee." She smiled, knowing he would.

Their favorite bench was near the road facing a waterway where several different types of birds, ducks and even an occasional crane made its home in the summer. While cars did drive by, almost no one stopped at this wonderful spot. They were most likely too much in a hurry to get somewhere else. After all, it was summer in The Hamptons.

"Troy, I've been replaying the interviews, trying to connect the damn clues, and I know we're missing something. Where did the murders actually happen? What happened to the clothes they had on before being stuffed into the Yellen dresses? And, needless to day, who committed the murders?"

"Oh yeah, minor detail," Troy replied, saying he was on his way

Troy hung up and grabbed the recent evidence report from Lara along with some photos she had handed to him earlier. He also had the magazine Marianna gave him that Jenna wanted to see.

Ten minutes later Troy and Jenna were huddling over the photos in that magazine.

"Troy, take a look at these photos. This event was just a little over a month ago." There was Alana Keller, Larson and Yellen's arms around her. On another page at a different event, there it was: Christian Keller, holding hands with—of all people—Nora Flynn.

"Well, we sure as hell could use an explanation from them." Troy turned the pages, looking for other photos of any of them. "Tomorrow we show Ms. Flynn these photos."

Now a little after five, Troy got up, walked to his car and headed home to Marianna and the kids.

Jenna and Watson walked back home, she gathered up a few things to take with her to Dave's, and they got into the jeep. She swore Watson had a smile on his face, or maybe it was just a reflection of *her* smile. Dave would be waiting for them.

***

Driving to Dave's, Jenna wondered aloud to Watson, "Where <u>are</u> Nora's boyfriend and her brother? Could one or both of them be involved with these murders?"

Nora had said she had not been able to reach them, but according to Nora, they sure found their way to her when they needed something.

CHAPTER 11

BACK TO THE
OYSTER BAR

"Dave, Watson and I will be at your place a little before six. I need to talk to the owner of the Oyster Bar. Let's get some dinner there. Okay?"

"See you soon," he said. "I'll be the hunk wearing the tight black t-shirt."

Dave was indeed a hunk to Jenna. They both knew the issue of marriage was hanging in the air.

Jenna knew she loved him. She didn't want to lose him. "Would he be willing to be patient about getting married?" she wondered.

Dave was waiting outside for her with serious flirtation in his eyes, and that said it all about his mood.

She had a huge smile on her face when she saw that and gave him the keys to Watson (meaning the leash) and told him, "I'll see Aggie later."

So that Dave and Jenna could go to dinner, Dave's assistant took over the care of Watson. Watson was rushing along, tail wagging, dragging the young man off to the rest of the setters in his care.

At the Oyster Bar, the owner took them to a table for two by the window so they could enjoy the wonderful view of sky and water. As locals and regulars, they got preferred treatment. Jenna showed the owner a few photos and asked him a few questions regarding the people in the photo, including: "Have any of these people been in together at any time in the past couple months?"

The owner's response truly surprised her. Jenna was nearly speechless: "Dave, I'm really sorry. I need to make a quick call to Troy. Then, dinnertime is ours, promise."

"Okay, but if you don't keep your promise, I'm keeping Watson permanently." He gave her that flirty look again. She didn't know what the heck he was up to.

She went outside and made the call: "Troy, Dave and I are at the Oyster Bar. I showed the owner the pictures of Nora, the ones we looked at earlier. He said he didn't recall seeing her in here with Yellen. She was, however, in here with someone else. Guess who that someone else was? Dr. Christian Keller!

"We need to talk to Nora tomorrow morning. I can be there by 9 A.M. See if Sergeant Miller can bring her in again. No more playing nice with her! Enough of her B.S.," announced Jenna. "See you in the morning at headquarters. Now it's time for me to pay attention to Dave or he threatened to take Watson away from me."

They ordered a wonderful, local white wine to go with a platter of fresh oysters and clams on the half shell, for which the Oyster Bar was known. Jenna sat back and listened to Dave talk about his plans for the Veterinary Center, with offices in the back and, eventually, a home for pets when their "parents" go away.

Dave and Jenna were never at a loss for conversation when they were together. They cared about so many of the same things. They laughed together and felt sad together. She wondered, "What in the world is stopping me from saying, 'Yes!' to our getting married?"

But she knew.

***

Aggie and Watson were snuggled together, asleep in Dave's Barn. It was the structure where the two Irish setters were born and eventually met their new parents for adoption.

"Too cute," smiled Jenna.

"So are you." Dave put his arm around her as they walked toward the house leaving the two Irish setters where they were for the night.

"I want to tell you something, Jenna," began Dave.

Jenna stopped. Her heart almost did, too. She was not ready for the marriage conversation—maybe after these murders were solved.

"I love you," Dave told her, "You know how I feel about you, how I feel about us. Sometimes, in life, you need to take a leap of faith."

Jenna leaned over and kissed Dave, telling him, "I love you, too. I'm scared about marriage. It's not easy to let go of one's history, but I'm working on it."

"I know."

"Let's go to bed," said Jenna, pulling Dave up and wrapping her arm around his waist.

"Wow, pushy broad," Dave laughed as they went into the bedroom.

***

Jenna and Dave found times alone were rare in the middle of the summer season. Dave had many city pet owners who needed a local vet, and, of course, there were people contacting Jenna for her discreet investigations.

One wife wanted her husband followed; one husband wanted his wife followed. The problem was they were married to each other! *"Charming* couple," she thought. Another couple wanted proof of people walking on their private beach at night. Jenna refused many of these types of requests. She considered them nuisance problems and explained she doesn't do those types of investigations.

She preferred doing work for Kristin's Environmental Law Firm, and working with Troy on criminal investigations (although murder seemed to be more than an occasional crime out here lately).

Even before she had gotten her PI license, there were times that she had helped Kristin Sterling with investigations. Now, that kind of work had increased as environmental issues became larger and broader on the East End.

Dave Carter, who had been breeding Irish setters for almost ten years, had also recently completed his studies and board exams to become a veterinarian. He was the romance in her life. Well, he was much more than that. Jenna had bought Watson a few years ago from Dave, and after a short time, it was love and romance for all three!

The three-year old Irish setter often sat on the floor of the car between her and Dave, and squished between their legs at dinner. At night, if they wanted alone time, they had to lock the bedroom door, but only after giving Watson an array of toys and treats. Still, Watson often went on interviews with her. After all, he was a very important part (the Watson to her Holmes) of her private investigating firm.

Murder, it seemed, followed her and Watson. Watson appeared to have a nose for it.

CHAPTER 12

SAVING THE PLOVERS

The small camera Jenna attached to one of the fences that had been built to protect the plovers had a sensor, which took photos of anyone who walked or drove by it. This was a wonderful gadget she had found in one of Manhattan's high-tech stores. She had been sure it would come in handy someday.

"How much more discreet can I be," she laughed when she bought it. After spending the night with Dave, and Watson spending it with Aggie, Jenna left Watson with them and went out to the plover site. She was to meet with Troy in the village mid-morning to determine their next moves regarding the "fashion" murder—or murders.

"Kristin, I know it's early, but I'm back at the plover site. I have photos of people who have been near the site the last couple days. Most of them are of teenagers, although it looks like one older, balding man, maybe in his sixties, is with them. I think they're the ones who have been hurting or harassing the birds," Jenna told her.

"Were any more killed?"

"No," Jenna replied. "It does look like someone's been trying to tear down a piece of the fence on one side. Also, there are a few photos of the remaining tire tracks from when the birds were killed."

"Do you think we can identify the people in those photos? If so, let's get these photos to the police."

"Absolutely. We should also be able to identify the type of vehicle that made the tracks. I'm on my way back to the police station regarding the Yellen and Larson murders. I'll email the photos to you, and I'm going to give a set to Sergeant Miller to see if he recognizes anyone. If it's the teenagers who are up to no good, Miller can email the photos to the police out East and see what they might know about the kids."

* * *

Less than a week later, three teenagers were arrested, two boys and a girl who had been arrested twice already this summer for being drunk and disorderly. The girl's uncle was also arrested. Killing the birds was considered a federal offence since the piping plover is an endangered species.

"Three rich kids and an arrogant uncle," Jenna told Kristin. "Rich and spoiled. Their parents demanded bail for the kids and their uncle, but the four of them were kept in jail overnight and told to be in court next week."

"Will anything be done to make them responsible?" asked Jenna.

"At the very least, they'll probably have to serve community time and pay a fine," Kristin replied.

Jenna thought surely that sense of entitlement often comes from their upbringing or lack of it.

"Let's ask one of the local papers to do a story to, at least, embarrass them," suggested Jenna. "The added joy of all this is that I'm sure to hear from His Majesty again, meaning, our senator."

"Great idea, I'll make a couple calls. Rich, spoiled and arrogant sounds familiar out here. Do let me know if you hear from the senator. Thanks again, Jenna. I appreciate this. Send the firm your bill."

On to the next—whatever that next is, thought Jenna.

***

Next wasn't far off.

Dave called Jenna upset and more furious than she had ever heard him: "A couple driving by a closed construction site saw a golden retriever tied to a fence and whimpering. They stopped, saw he needed help and brought him here last night. He had no food or water, probably for several days. He was in such bad condition that we had to put him to sleep.

"The couple also had taken photos of the poor dog lying there. The name of the firm was in the background. I'm calling the papers and sending them the photos. Every year this happens. It's damn cruel and has to stop."

CHAPTER 13

BLACKMAIL

Well, at least no new bodies have appeared.

However, Tom Overton and Patrick Flynn were still missing. Troy decided to have Sergeant Miller run them through the system to see what specifics might be available about them.

Miller walked into Johnson's office. "Sir, turns out Overton's been arrested several times. He has started fights at a couple of the local bars, beat up a girlfriend a few years back and was fired from one of his jobs for stealing money. Somehow he always got out of doing any jail time by agreeing to community service. Here's his rap sheet and photo."

"What about Flynn, Nora's brother?"

Sergeant Miller placed another rap sheet on the detective's desk and then sat down in front of him stretching out his legs. "Seems he's even worse. He spent three years in jail back in Oklahoma where he grew up for running someone over, almost a rival gang situation. Then he moved here. Nora has bailed him out of bar brawls, same as Overton. Interesting side note: Flynn still has a driver's license and car. Overton does not."

"Do we know how long they have been in this area?"

"Apparently Flynn has been here only a couple of years. He gives his sister's address as his. Overton has been here much longer, going on eight years, and has a small apartment over on the North Fork." Miller continued looking at the reports adding, "We need to get his address

72

from Nora and check out his place. We should also find out from her what kind of car her brother drives and see where that might be."

"I want her in here as soon as possible," said Troy. "She knows a damn lot more than she's telling us."

***

"They're both bad guys, Nora," Johnson sat down and showed her the police reports on both of them.

Although Nora had a scarf wrapped around her shoulders, she was shivering: "I have no idea where either of them are, they never even returned my calls. I'm scared that maybe something has happened to them."

Nora still looked as if she had slept in the clothes she had on the day before. She had bitten off her nails, although she apparently had washed off her makeup and combed her hair. As she sat across from Jenna and Troy, Nora just kept shaking her head as if she was saying, "No, no, no."

Jenna leaned over towards Nora, and in a very stern voice told her, "We're hoping that your boyfriend or your brother aren't dead! The police are trying to find them, Nora. Now, *right now*, give Sergeant Miller your boyfriend's address. Plus, we want the make and color of your brother's car. And damn it Nora, I do mean *now*."

Nora practically whispered the information to the Sergeant. She was scared, overwhelmed, and knew things were about to get worse. Only she had no idea how much worse!

Then, Detective Johnson showed Nora some photos of her with Dr. Keller. "Care to explain?"

Nora covered her mouth, closed her eyes, and took a deep breath. After a minute, she seemed to recover and reached into her bag to pull out her recorder.

Jenna sat back in her chair, watching Nora set a small, old fashioned, tape recorder on the table, "I made this the night I stayed at the house of my friend, Cate Ashton. It explains the truth about the gown and Dr. Keller.

"During our last interview, I asked you if I should I get an attorney. Then I went home and called Dr. Keller. Something in the way he responded scared me a lot, which was why I went to Cate's and made

73

this recording. It explains everything you want to know about the gown and Mr. Yellen."

"Do you know who murdered him and Kevin Larson?" Jenna asked.

"I'm not sure. I do know I didn't kill either of them."

Nora pushed Play on the recorder.

***

The tape began with, "It was Dr. Keller's idea. We've been having an affair the past year. About a month ago, he asked me to push Andre Yellen to donate that gown to the fundraiser. That was the one I bid on. He gave me a photo to show Mr. Yellen."

"Then what?" Detective Johnson and Jenna sat back in the windowless interrogation room, letting Nora finally tell the truth. Hopefully!

"He told me how to play up to Yellen, what to say and how to go about convincing him by stroking his ego. He also suggested using very negative comments about both Dr. Kellers. Keller said Yellen would love hearing that. He gave me a ticket to the event, a check to deposit into my account to pay for the gown and $2,500 cash."

Nora looked up at them as the story of her and Keller's duplicity in this crime began to unfold on the tape.

The tape recording continued with Nora's voice: "Dr. Keller told me to say the idea was Andre Yellen's, to mislead the police. After I was at the station and asked if I needed an attorney, I called and told him what was happening. He said he would be over later. He sounded so weird that I got really scared, so I called him back and told him he had better not. I said that the house was probably being watched by the police."

Nora was crying continuously as the tape played for them. It was difficult to feel any sympathy for her. She had lied, misled the investigation and who knows what else? However, Jenna and Troy didn't think she had committed the murders.

"I did all Dr. Keller asked. I don't know how and why Mr. Yellen was killed, and I certainly never had anything to do with Mr. Larson. I didn't even know him. I asked Dr. Keller about the murders and he said not to worry, everything would be fine. Well, everything wasn't fine 'cause when I came home from Cate's, I had to call the police! Someone had broken into my house and left a threatening message on my living room wall."

"Nora," Jenna added sarcastically. "Does Keller know you made this tape? Also, did anyone else know about this scheme?"

"Yes. I told Dr. Keller I was giving it to you today and to stay away from me because I was frightened about everything that happened. He said if I gave you this tape, he would say I lied and it was all my idea to get money from him."

"And who else knew?" Jenna was demanding an answer.

"Yeah. Tom Overton and my brother both knew I had some extra money. When I offered to help Patrick pay for some auto repairs, he asked me where I suddenly got so much money. I told him I did some work for Dr. Keller apart from being his assistant."

"Then what did they do?" Jenna rolled her eyes and took a drink of water. "Stop stalling. We need to know the whole damn truth here, Nora."

"I'm trying to do that," she whispered.

Detective Johnson stood up and leaned against the wall, arms crossed, and told her to tell them about her brother and boyfriend's actions once they knew she had extra money from Dr. Keller.

"They left together right away and said they were going to see if they could do some work for the good doctor. I haven't seen either of them since!" Nora put her head in her hands and sobbed.

Detective Johnson was already on his phone asking Sergeant Miller to put Nora Flynn in a jail cell. For now, she was under arrest for complicity regarding one murder and misleading a murder investigation. Besides, because Troy wished he could include that he found her damn annoying!

Jenna pushed a box of tissues over to her. "Nora, we are going to need your help to bring them in once we know where they are. Are you willing to do that? It could make a big difference in what happens to you."

Nora nodded yes, wiping her eyes and nose with the tissues, while getting up to be led to jail. Jenna followed her out of the room. Jenna wanted to talk to Troy privately.

"Troy, whoever did these murders had to be bigger, stronger than Nora in order to dress them and move their bodies."

"You bet, like her brother and boyfriend. But I doubt they had the brains to come up with this whole scheme on their own. I'm pretty sure those two were involved, but their rap sheets show a couple of losers and users."

CHAPTER 14

COMPUTER
FORENSICS

Jenna surprised James Parker when she approached him.

"So, James, how would you like to quit your job as a security guard? Between the police department and me, we can probably hire you at least twenty hours a week: Ten for the police department, and ten, sometimes even more for me. Troy and his captain have been talking to Lara for months now about expanding the lab services and capabilities, which would require someone with a specialty in Computer Forensics. In fact, they've been told it would not only be useful here, but also in some of the other smaller communities in the state."

"Are you serious?" James looked at Jenna and she was sure she noticed a bit of the sadness in his eyes going away (or, maybe she was just hoping she could help make that happen).

"Absolutely. Lara said she needed someone who had the skills to set up the program and oversee it. She had funds approved for it months ago. As long as you pass a background check, are not wanted by the police and have no prison record, you're it!"

It took James all of twenty minutes to resign as a security guard.

After James Parker had lost his leg, an army therapist had suggested to him: "Keep a journal. It's a way of giving voice to your thoughts and feelings and not holding them all inside of you."

Some days he did, when he was especially sad, remembering the bad things, the awful times after they took away part of his leg. Sometimes he didn't write in it for months. Today was different, very different.

"Life is full of unexpected turns and developments. When least expected, there are new beginnings. Now new hopes seemed to have appeared. My life has been so wrapped up in sadness and pain, so I want to believe this is real. I think it is. I start a new job tomorrow. I met a very nice lady I will be working with. Her name is Lara Stern. I also met another nice lady I'll be working for. Her name is Jenna Preston. She's a private investigator."

James Parker did indeed find himself in the most unexpected of circumstances due to murder. Certainly not one he had committed!

The first time he had met Lara Stern at the police forensic lab, she showed him the x-rays of the two murdered celebrities, Andre Yellen and Kevin Larson. "James, it seems the world of beauty has been seriously disfigured. These stab wounds in the neck, on each of them it's the same. See if your computer program can generate illustrations of what type of knife was used."

***

Troy went back to his office, a couple of murders didn't stop other crimes from happening in The Hamptons. There was trespassing, beach noise and parking complaints for him and Sergeant Miller to handle. Miller also continued to deal with the press about the murders.

"Miller, you keep the media updated. I'm afraid if they keep poking at us, I might commit a justified murder myself. Mostly, say, 'We're working on it.'"

Jenna watched as James did what she called computer stuff, researching different types of knives, their shapes, blades, mixing and matching them.

Lara was also watching him as he maneuvered the computer. "James, this is brilliant. Can you do this with the rope or whatever strangled them?"

"The murderer took the knife and rope and hid them somewhere. If we can identify types, we can backtrack to where they might have been bought," Jenna added. She was now standing closer to the computer screen, watching images enlarged on Lara's equipment, mesmerized by the whole process.

Within fifteen minutes, James Parker had helped identified the type of knife and blade, and places in the area that sold them. He would need more time for what had been used to strangle the two men. Lara printed out the information, handing it to Jenna. Meantime, she had moved ever so slightly closer to James.

It seemed to be an enticing new beginning for both James and Lara.

Jenna told the two of them, "Keep at it. I'm going to show this to Detective Johnson. Let us know if you have anything else. Great job, you two."

It was all a unique moment in time for Lara and James. She had been married, once, over fifteen years ago. He had been killed in a freak biking accident right after their Third Anniversary. "It broke my heart, I buried him and never discussed it again until now," Lara told all this to Jenna a few weeks after James began working with her. Closely!

James had family in Virginia. His parents were alive and he had a younger brother and an older sister. Limping, sad, feeling like a failure; he had been too embarrassed to be around them. He couldn't stand being the object of their pitying looks.

So, James came north, not sure what he would do, what he would find. He had been grateful for the job as a security guard. It helped him pay the rent and had given him time to work out some of his computer ideas.

Now his life was different, very different.

James and Lara liked each other: A lot!

James wrote in his journal a couple months later: *"Is it possible? Really, is it possible?"*

***

James smiled when Jenna told him about the rest of her investigation staff—they of course being Watson and Aggie. She also said she wanted him to meet Dave and his other setters. Her thoughts had been that she and James could set up an office at Dave's. He would have plenty of space in the new veterinary center.

James knew he would have to explain to all of them about his having PTSD and what that was like for him. But he knew his new friends, actually a new and different type of family, would be understanding and supportive.

He would discover they certainly were.

CHAPTER 15

VENGEANCE

Dr. Eric Gold, a New York psychiatrist, was doing his best to explain the irrational mind and actions of someone who feels they need to *get even* with someone, or even a particular group of people: "For some reason, they have made a given situation larger than life by their inability to cope with a loss, a hurt, a sadness, or a betrayal—whether real or justified. The truth is that they may be experiencing a great deal of self-hatred or self-pity that they direct towards these other people."

Jenna had met Dr. Gold several years ago at a holiday party in her parents' home. Both he and her father were on the board of a New York City hospital. She was really desperate for some insight into the kind of person or persons who committed the Yellen and Larson murders, so Jenna had called him. Jenna was pretty sure he would be willing to discuss the problem with her. After all, her father's influence was quite extensive; and, well, she needed a little help here.

"It isn't rational," Dr. Gold told her, "but they make it their life's mission to exact punishment, a type of retribution, on someone they believed had caused them great harm or a great loss. Vengeance is a violent reaction. It's revenge to the extreme."

"I know you can't say anything about the particular individuals involved, but what makes someone snap twenty or thirty years after the supposed harmful incident?" Jenna was on the phone with Dr. Gold for almost an hour already. If her family hadn't known him, Jenna figured she would probably owe him a day's pay. He was a rather prominent, sought after psychiatrist, especially with the more wealthy people of Manhattan.

"Jenna, you're looking for rational answers for irrational acts."

"I know, I know. So, do you think the murders of Andre Yellen and Kevin Larson were extreme acts of revenge for old wounds and maybe even some new ones? Of course, it seems to me, from what you're saying, that it's more likely to be the old wounds, ones they built out of proportion to reality. Now these 'victims' have been driven to violent acts of murder." Jenna was switching the phone from one ear to the other while Dr. Gold did his best explain to her the destructive personality that led to this type of behavior."

"Think about this, Jenna. How often have we heard of young men carrying out acts of violence against their own classmates or teachers? All too often they have been abused or abandoned. They've been so badly mistreated they want to hurt someone else as badly as they believe they've been hurt. How about someone who kills their boss who had good reason to fire them? It didn't matter to the aggrieved person. An irrationally thinking mind can rationalize reasons for committing such irrational and often unspeakable acts. Something can trigger that behavior at any time."

"Even after many years?"

"Yes, in fact, often after many years. Jenna, in your line of work, you've probably met them many times. They're compulsive gamblers or liars. They might be stealing money from employers or otherwise exhibiting deceitful behaviors. Worst of all, they can express uncontrollable anger or rage at any time."

"So, is murder the result of anger or rage?"

"Worse. That is what Buddhism calls violence in the mind. For some reason, these thoughts have become uncontrollable and have pushed that person into believing they are entitled to revenge. They believe it's their right."

Jenna realized she liked Dr. Gold. His sense of clarity and honestly was comforting in the midst of this craziness. She thanked him and commented: "It's ironic, of course, that jails are full of people who were sure they were making the right decision to commit such acts. They believe that they were justified, and yet, their own lives are cut off, and they are left with little meaning and less hope."

***

She told Troy, and later Dave, about her conversation with Dr. Gold: "I understand what he was explaining, and I think it's very alarming. You never know when someone is going to suddenly decide it's time for retribution. He said that there are warning signs; such as the less violent, yet still destructive, acts of cheating, lying, stealing and gambling. Such a person may show excessive anger at times over minor incidents.

"I believe that this is really a case of extreme vengeance in the form of retribution. They wanted the whole world to witness what happened to them. Whoever wanted these two men murdered seems to have lost almost complete control of their own actions."

Troy leaned back, rubbing the back of his neck as he looked up at her. While playing, his young children often hung on him and were the source of frequent neck aches and pains. "Jenna, okay, let's review what we know. In a written statement, Alana said she was leaving Christian. Larson had promised he was going to put her in the next couple of movies he was producing, which of course turned out to be B.S. That was enough for her to have been very angry at him."

"Pretty dumb for someone who's supposed to be smart and successful."

Troy continued, both rubbing his neck and going over the case with Jenna.

"Before she realized it was B.S., Alana Keller told her husband the marriage was over, and she was going to be in the movies wearing clothes designed by Yellen. That would certainly make him go over the edge, thinking that Yellen had agreed to design the clothes for her to wear in the films. She told her husband Yellen had even promised he would remake the gown for her that he had originally designed specifically for her years ago. That was the one auctioned off at the recent fundraiser. Then it was stolen, and Yellen was stuffed into it."

"Yes, Troy, but remember there is even more to that gown story. It was originally designed as a wedding dress for Alana's marriage to

Christian. They had hired a high-priced publicist who had sent out announcements about it to the style and gossip columnists all over Manhattan. I believe Patricia found a couple of those mentioned in back issues of lifestyle columns. I'll get her to email them to us."

Troy was on a roll. "However, before she had the chance to wear it, Yellen and Christian had a huge business fight, which cost the Kellers a lot of money to extricate themselves from that relationship. When it was done, Yellen then sent photos of the gown, worn by a gorgeous model, to the society pages of papers and fashion magazines. It made the Kellers look like liars and even worse for them, they felt like fools, according to some articles I read."

"Wow, you've got the story in order. How crazy—to commit two murders for what happened so many years ago," Jenna was rubbing *her* head now. It was contagious. "This damn case is giving me a headache."

"So, from your conversation with Dr. Gold, do you really think this nonsense about this gown could actually make one or both of them be driven to murder?" Troy was getting exasperated at the entire affair.

"I think so, Troy. Both Dr. Kellers were furious at the time. Yellen obviously meant them to be very embarrassed. Their social world was buzzing about Yellen making what was supposed to be a one-of-a kind gown for Alana. In addition, besides the business financial losses, they had paid thousands of dollars for Yellen to make that one-of-a-kind dress especially for Dr. Alana Christian."

"You know, Jenna, Christian Keller certainly had some big gambling loses over the years. The report we got about his finances showed he had a major problem. For one thing, there were lots of big payments to bookies. Fortunately for him, he also made a lot of money doing cosmetic surgery on wealthy people.

***

Over the years, unhappy and disillusioned with her marriage, Alana Keller attempted to get even with her husband by sleeping with both Larson and Yellen. Meantime, Dr. Christian Keller couldn't care less, according to articles in the local rags. In addition to gambling debts, he had numerous affairs. Many of the couple's battles and affairs had been played out on the gossip pages. It was likely they had only stayed together for the money they made by referring patients to each other's practices.

They had spent a lifetime being miserable with each other.

Soon it was about to get much worse.

CHAPTER 16

DOUBLE TROUBLE

Inside Mary's Local Bar (yes, that's the name of it), Tom Overton and Patrick Flynn were flying high. As they bragged about their good fortune, they slapped each other on the back and gave each other high-fives.

"Come on man, let's go to Mexico when we finish this job. We'll have plenty of money. There's lots of good looking broads and great booze down there." Laughing and very plastered, Tom was telling this brilliant idea to Patrick.

Patrick, now almost as drunk as Tom, slapped him another high five at his idea. "Yeah, smart to get out of here. Hey, watch out for my sister. She'll want to get married and make you settle down. Who needs that shit?"

"You ain't kidding. I sure as hell don't want to get married, not to her or anyone."

"Only another week, buddy, and we'll be in the money, ready to rock and roll out of this place," Patrick said as he slid off his bar stool and headed to the bathroom.

The two kept complimenting each other on their brilliant scheme, the money they would have to do anything they wanted and how they were getting away with murder.

***

"They went on acting like a couple of jackasses for a couple hours until they tried to buy drinks for everyone in here. I stopped that. They got pissed at me and left. Thank goodness!" Mary, owner of the Local Bar on the North Fork, poured Jenna a soda.

"Any idea where they went when they left here?"

"Nope, and I didn't ask. You know they could be brothers. They look a lot alike, almost the same height and same color hair. They were both wearing cheap jeans and concert t-shirts."

Jenna was sipping her soda: "Could you tell if they were right or left handed?"

"Nope. Besides, when they didn't have a beer in each hand, they were either slapping each other on the back or giving those ridiculous high-fives every time they mentioned the money they were getting. The only difference I could tell between them was Tom's back was slightly bent over, not the other guy."

"If they come back, I would appreciate a call. The police and I would like to talk to these two characters."

Jenna finished her soda, put a couple of dollars on the bar and handed her card to Mary.

"Thanks, Mary. Appreciate your help."

***

Mary Bennett called Jenna to tell her that Overton and Flynn had been at the bar again: "Those two you asked about. They were both here a little after noon. No more slaps on the back. They looked real scared if you ask me. Flynn kept asking if someone would take them to Southampton, where he said he left his car. I finally told them to call a damn taxi, same as they got here."

"Did they?" Jenna asked sliding onto a bar stool.

"Sure. But I also heard Flynn calling his sister for help. He told her they needed a ride to the city and that they had to get out of here fast." Mary brought a card over with the name of a taxi company she used to come pick up drunks at the bar.

"Their behavior was like two crazy guys on dope. They seemed so wired, but you kind of get used to it. There's always a few drunks and weirdos hanging out in a bar like this."

Mary was putting peanuts and chips out on the bar and opening beers for a couple of customers, while a waitress was wiping up the tables. Jenna looked at her and smiled. She liked this woman. Smart, no nonsense, and her tone suggested she had certainly been around and could easily spot losers like Overton and Flynn.

Mary Bennett was in her early forties, about 5'6", green eyes and long dark blonde hair. She owned the bar for about eight years. At first she was a barmaid, then a waitress, and then the manager, before buying the bar dirt cheap from the previous owner who just wanted out.

Before all that, she was homeless. She had talked about it with Jenna, who started coming in a couple of times a week; sometimes for lunch, sometimes just to say hello and get a soda. One time, Mary opened up about having been homeless and talked about the issue of homelessness on the East End of Long Island.

"People think because it's The Hamptons, no one here is poor or homeless, when in fact there's plenty of it. There are homeless men and women—even children—who live on church steps, in cardboard homes under bridges or sleep on the street. Those who have a car usually sleep in it and pray their locked doors will keep them safe. That was me, for eight months, until I was lucky enough to get a job here at this bar. The owner was a good guy and gave me a chance. I sure as hell wasn't going to disappoint him."

"I know, Mary, I saw homeless people when I was living in Manhattan. All too often they're ignored by the people walking by them, or they look at them with disgust."

"Believe me, Jenna, I know only too well."

"I like you, Mary Bennett. You have both courage and heart."

"By the way, Jenna, your senator sure is no help to those in need, unless it's *his* needs. We've asked for help with homeless shelters and even providing some places for food pantries.

"His answer was 'No.'"

"What a jerk he is!" Jenna told her, "Even without his help, we could probably do something. First we need to solve this case."

CHAPTER 17

THE SENATOR PROBLEM—AGAIN

Senator Lawrence Thomas Quinn certainly did not care about the homeless. He cared only about the big-money people who paid big bucks so that the senator could win his campaigns and do what they wanted him to do.

The senator loved being in the limelight. He loved himself more than anything. His ego was the size of the entire country and his substance the size of a pea. Most of his constituents would tell you that.

Dark brown hair, deep brown eyes, Quinn was a little over 5'10," with more than a hint of a belly over his belt. He always wore clothes that had someone else's name on them such as Lauren, Gucci and Armani.

Lawrence Thomas Quinn, now in his second term, definitely owed his career as a senator to campaign money from the rich. Some were wealthy homeowners with huge second homes in The Hamptons, while others were business owners with East End interests. They continually told the senator, "Keep those crazy environmentalists away from our businesses and our homes, and we'll keep you in office."

Yes, the good senator had been bought and paid for, so he did his benefactors' bidding when asked. Most of them sure as hell did not like those plovers nesting on *their beach* and told him in stern voices, "Tell those damn environmentalists to stay out of our way or else!"

Or else what?

***

Once again the senator asked—well, more like told—Jenna, "Meet me at the coffee café in an hour. We need to discuss the problem."

Jenna figured it was best to humor him so she could find out what was annoying his majesty (as she and Kristin called him) and his wealthy patrons *now*. It was also a chance to mention the homeless issue on the East End and see how he responded (not that she expected anything positive from him on that front).

Jenna found him waiting for her at a corner table inside, sitting with his legs crossed and sockless feet in expensive loafers. He was dressed in his summer cream-colored linen pants and a Lauren polo shirt. He was drinking a fancy coffee.

"Jenna, those damn plovers are causing a big headache for some of the homeowners, and now—arresting their kids! What nonsense is that?"

"Thanks, senator, nice to see you, too. Why, yes, I would love a coffee."

"Stop the wisecracks with me, Jenna, you know those plovers are a problem, and they could nest somewhere else. Why do they have to do it on our beaches?"

"You have to be kidding. Like you think they purposely picked these beaches because they know it's The Hamptons? Those kids killed the plovers. That's illegal. Go fight the law, not me and the environmentalists." Jenna was speaking a bit loud intentionally. Trying to enjoy their coffee and sweet treats, other patrons turned and looked at the two of them.

The senator shot back: "Quiet down. I can hear you. So can the whole coffee shop! Look, some kids behaved badly. They're sorry, they won't do it again."

"Hey, I'm not the law. I told you, what they did is against the law. They committed a crime. Aren't you supposed to help uphold the law?"

"I'm taking care of the people who live out here, not some damn birds." The senator was red in the face, doing his best to hold back his great annoyance at Jenna. He realized that the entire café audience was now staring at both of them.

"Well senator, some of the people out here—that you say you take care of—are very concerned about those birds. What about *them*?" Jenna raised her eyebrows with intentional implication and got up to get her own coffee.

The senator was sitting with his right leg over his left. The top leg swung up and down because he was now ready to explode. Of course, knowing they were in a very public place, he waited until Jenna sat back down, and then he practically hissed at her: "I'm going to have your licensed revoked."

"For what? Disobeying you? Come on, you know the law is not with those rich kids and their parents. Senator, they're just going to have to deal with the consequences of their actions. You can go back and tell them you tried . . .

Jenna took another swipe at him: "Oh, by the way, why have you refused to help find funding for the homeless needs on the East End?"

Once again, Senator Quinn glared at Jenna as he often did in one of these meetings with her. He knew he had met his match. She was smart and—damn it—she knew how to aggravate the hell out of him. He kept to himself the fact that he was well aware of her parents, the Prestons, in New York. He thought he might want to be governor one day, and they could be very useful.

If Quinn ever told that to Jenna Preston, chances are she would have broken out in laughter at the absurdity of it.

Senator Lawrence Thomas Quinn got up, without answering her question about the homeless, and walked out.

The girl behind the pastry counter yelled out, "Senator, you forgot to pay."

***

CHAPTER 18

FOUND

Overton and Flynn were hiding out in the windmill building, just blocks from the Larson house where Yellen's body had been found. The windmill was not meant for living or hiding.

A local landmark, the windmill had not worked for over thirty years. Nonetheless, it was an icon and connected one Hamptons village to another. It sat in the middle of landscaped property, which was maintained by the two villages it connected. It was a wonderful reminder for locals of when The Hamptons was less hectic, before so much wealth permeated its shores, all too often causing harm to its quality of life.

Patrick and Tom were in a state of extreme panic. They had come to realize that their plans for lots of money and life South of the Border were about to take them straight to a life in prison.

The two of them were now reaching out to Nora as their savior, the very same Nora they were about to leave behind to pursue what they had high-fived about recently, "broads and beer." These were the big ambitions for their lives.

"Broads and beer! We're a couple of young guys who wanna have fun. We don't wanna be tied down to sixty-hours-a-week jobs and married to someone with a house and kids. That's for suckers."

Mary had told Jenna this was one of the conversations she had overheard when the two men were at the bar the week before. That was a week before the whole scheme was about to come crashing down on them!

***

"Nora, it's Patrick and Tom. We need your help. We're in trouble. I left my car at the Southampton train station, cause we was planning to go to the city, and when we were walking into town Dr. Keller saw us. I tell you, he was acting like a crazy man."

The police had told Nora: "We're letting you go, but we'll be outside watching you at your home. We expect your brother and boyfriend will contact you to help them now that they know they're in big trouble. You're to call Jenna as soon as you hear from them. She'll drive you to wherever they are, and we'll follow right behind the two of you."

Nora nodded in agreement. The good doctor had already gotten her in plenty of hot water already. She had every intention of doing what Jenna and the police told her to do.

Patrick was yelling into the phone: "Nora, please come get me and Tom. Dr. Keller pulled over when he saw us, got out of his car and screamed at us. He called us 'just a couple of stupid idiots.' The S.O.B. said he told the police we killed them and that I had I blackmailed him for I don't know why, some reason. I punched him hard, and I'm pretty sure he has a broken nose! He's a damn liar. He's the one who murdered those two queens. We're not stupid! We have proof in the trunk of my car. Don't tell anyone where we are. We'll run right out and get into your car, so you can drive us to NYC."

***

While the police were outside her drab home filled with its sad memories, Nora Flynn called Jenna to tell her she had gotten the phone call from her brother that they had expected.

"He said he and Tom are hiding out in the village windmill, and they're going to wait for me to pick them up. Patrick said Dr. Keller killed both Yellen and Larson, and they have proof in his car."

Jenna had been waiting for the call. She was nearby and told Nora she would be there in five minutes. "Meantime, call your brother back,

93

and tell him you'll be there in about twenty minutes because you have to borrow a friend's car. Say that your car can't get them to the city because it broke down yesterday."

Nora did as she was told and then waited outside in her driveway. She stood leaning against her car, wearing a worn-looking pink sweater, jeans, t-shirt and sneakers. She had no makeup, but apparently she did brush her hair for the occasion.

Jenna pulled up and told Nora: "Hurry up, get in, the police will follow us. They've already called Detective Troy Johnson to meet us there. We have to expect the unexpected. We don't know if they have weapons, but we do know they're dangerous. They've been involved in two murders."

Jenna waited for Nora to climb into her jeep and slam the door shut. Then Nora sat quietly next to Watson as the three of them drove off to capture Nora's brother and boyfriend.

Referring to her companion squeezed in between them, Jenna said, "Watson is with us, just in case. He can be very protective when necessary." There really was nothing else for either of them to say at this point. Nora was in the middle of one big mess.

Jenna had no illusion this would be easy. These two guys were rightfully scared. They had been accomplices to murder. Once they were captured, they would be spending a lot of time in jail. However, if Dr. Christian Keller was indeed the killer and the mastermind behind the whole sordid series of events, he was hopefully going to be put away for much longer. Jenna was pretty damn sure that would be the case.

When they got near the windmill, Nora looked at her with a tearful face filled with emotion. "Jenna, they will see I'm not alone when we get there."

"That's okay. They need to realize it's over for them."

***

Both Tom and Patrick came running out of the entrance to the windmill. As expected, they screamed at Nora when they noticed the police cars had also pulled right behind car she came in.

"You bitch! You betrayed us!" shouted Tom Overton.

"Patrick, please, they will have to shoot you if you try to run away," Nora pleaded with her brother and ran towards him. He was family. Then, he realized it was useless to do anything but surrender. Patrick held up his hands, got down on his knees and sobbed as Nora went over to him, held him and cried with him.

Meantime, Jenna had gotten out of her jeep, and she started after Tom Overton. Watson and one of the police officers were right behind her. Overton was running down the winding, sandy road toward the beach when he saw someone getting into a car. Overton pulled him away from it, tossed him on the ground and began a chase for his life in the stolen car. The poor car owner didn't know what the hell had happened until much later.

After darting back to the jeep, Jenna and Watson led a chase after him through beach roads and side streets. He led them around the back roads and side streets of the villages for almost an hour, often going the wrong way on one-way roads and banging into parked cars. Finally, he drove down a dead end beach road, which was a dead end in more ways than one for Tom Overton. Still, he wasn't ready to give up; not just yet.

Two police cars, one with Detective Johnson, had followed and joined in the chase. Overton jumped out of the car and ran towards the backyard of one of the large—well, very large—homes. Jenna and Watson ran after him. Daylight was moving toward dusk and now they had to capture Overton before darkness made it easier for him to hide—or possibly escape.

Troy got out of his car and quickly caught up with Jenna and Watson. The three of them rushed together into the back yard. The homeowners came outside, were obviously stunned, and left wondering what was going on at their home.

"We can explain to them later, Jenna! Let's get this creep!"

Watson had run ahead of them and was barking. Jenna and Troy literally screeched to a stop as they reached the backyard with its huge swimming pool. There was Tom Overton floundering around with Watson threatening to nip him.

"Get this damn dog away from me," screamed Overton. "He wants to bite off my face."

Suppressing a grin, Jenna glanced at Troy. She told Overton, "I'm not sure I can stop him, but I'll try. You'll have to stay in the water until I calm him down."

Troy had to look the other way for fear he would crack up at Jenna's comments. Still, he couldn't help laughing at the site of the fool flopping around around the pool like a fish trying to avoid getting caught. Of course, eventually, Jenna pulled Watson back. Two police officers came and dragged Overton out of the pool, handcuffed him and stuck him, dripping wet, into the back of one of the police cars. They did throw him a towel!

Overton was indeed under arrest, as was Patrick Flynn.

It soon became apparent that not only was there plenty of evidence against Overton and Flynn, but there was also plenty in the trunk of Patrick Flynn's car to incriminate Dr. Christian Keller.

Keller's broken nose from his earlier run in with Overton and Flynn was about to be the least of his concerns!

CHAPTER 19

EVIDENCE

Lara was reviewing the evidence found on Flynn and Overton when they were captured. "Believe me, there is plenty of incriminating evidence here on these two guys, plus there's fingerprints from a third person."

Jenna, Troy, Sergeant Miller and James Parker stood quietly in the state-of-the-art lab as Lara went over the specifics including what she had found in Flynn's car.

Nora Flynn had told Detective Johnson that her brother's car was at the Hampton train station. "He told me it was packed and ready for a getaway. He also said that he and Tom had saved evidence to protect themselves from someone who had hired them to help kill Mr. Yellen and Mr. Larson."

After the pair was arrested and the car was towed to the police station garage, Sergeant Miller informed Detective Johnson and Jenna, "Flynn was in possession of close to a thousand dollars stuffed into the glove compartment. There was also a stash of recreational drugs and, catch this, the clothes the two of them had on when they helped murder Yellen. Blood spatter was all over the front of the shirts and pants that they had put in a black plastic garbage bag and stuffed in the trunk."

"These guys really thought they could get away with this," Jenna was shaking her head, clearly dumbfounded at their dumb behavior.

"Okay. Here's the jackpot," James interrupted. "The clothes Yellen and Larson had been wearing before they were murdered were also in the trunk of his Flynn's car. Lara said the evidence and a third set of fingerprint clearly points to Dr. Christian Keller. His fingerprints are on the clothes that were pulled off the victims as well as on the Yellen gowns that both victims were wearing when they were found."

"We also discovered bloodstains, fibers, and a couple of bottles of that black polish in the trunk of Patrick Flynn's car with Flynn's and Overton's fingerprints on all over it," Lara told them.

Troy turned and looked at Jenna with a grin. Lara and James had become quite a team in a very short time.

"The evidence against Keller and those two morons should put them all away for a long time. Nice work, you two!" Troy was gathering the bagged and labeled evidence, getting it ready to show both of the Keller's attorneys.

James turned to Lara and smiled.

"Lara was almost blushing," thought Jenna. "Wow!"

Troy noticed, looked at Jenna and smiled.

Sergeant Miller turned and looked at Lara and James. "Murder and romance, quite a combination," he whispered to Jenna as he walked out, quietly laughing.

***

Gotcha!

Troy shoved the pictures of the two murdered men in front of Patrick Flynn and Tom Overton: "Whose idea was it to murder them?"

"It was Dr. Keller, Nora's boss," said Tom Overton, arrogantly. He was literally doing all the talking for the two of them, blaming everyone, and typically owning none of the blame himself.

Pale and silent, Flynn kept his head down.

"Patrick and I went to Keller after we saw Nora had extra cash, which he had given her to help him. She didn't say for what, but we figured there had to be a way for us to get in on that action."

"Did you call him first or just show up at his office? Troy asked him.

"We called first. I told him who we were and that we wanted to meet him or we would tell his wife he was cheating with Nora... which Patrick and I kinda knew 'cause we saw them going out together one night when we were staying at her house."

"Did you talk to him that night?" Jenna was thinking they were more like *freeloading* at Nora's house.

"Nah, we was already wasted on beer Nora had in the house. Anyhow, he looked at us quiet-like for a minute. Then he got this weird smile on his face and said that he had a great idea of a way we could help him."

"Help him do what?" Jenna stared right at him, with Troy next to her doing the same. Both of them were unable to believe what an idiot this guy was and that he actually seemed to be bragging!

"Help him get rid of a couple of guys giving him a lot of trouble."

"Okay, so he asked you to help him *basically kill people.* Then what?" asked Troy, as he noticed that Overton, who had been sitting still, was finally squirming a bit.

"This Keller dude told us where to buy a couple of blond wigs and black polish. Said he would tell me what to do with them and that he wanted to meet again the next day. Then he gave Patrick a thousand dollars cash. I figured, 'What a fool!' A thousand bucks just to go shopping for him!"

"And the next day?" Troy snapped.

"The next day we met at his office after hours, like he told us. We brought the two blond wigs and polish. He showed us a photo of the first guy he wanted us to set up to get axed, and then, the second guy he wanted killed. Then, he told us exactly what we was to do."

"Did he tell you Nora had a gown you had to get from her?" Jenna picked up a warm diet soda, sipping it, looking at them, nodding to keep him talking.

"Yeah. He said that Nora would have some gown we're supposed to dress the guy in after he's dead. He told us what time to pick it up and even to hit her on the head when she was at her front door. Hey, for all that money, what's a bump on the head to the broad?"

"But it seems as if you didn't expect Keller to be at Nora's when you did that. Were you surprised he was there?" Jenna asked.

"Very surprised! He had been hiding off to the side of the house when we got there. And we were even more surprised when we saw him stick a needle in back of her neck, *after* we already hit her. He said it was to knock her out until morning. Then we dragged her into the house and left her on the living room floor. She had been concentrating on getting into her house with the gown so she didn't even realize we were all hiding there."

Jenna got up, thinking she wanted to smack this idiot, knowing she wouldn't—well, actually, legally she couldn't.

When Flynn and Overton were booked, the police obtained a fresh set of prints from both of them. These prints clearly matched the prints on the polish and tossed clothes that were found. Lara and Troy knew they had their evidence, but now they wanted the story. Most of all, they wanted to be ready so that, when meeting with Keller, they could push him for a confession.

Jenna whispered to Troy, "Bet you Keller blames everything on these two."

Overton continued the story leaning back in his chair, while Patrick still didn't say a word.

"Keller had told us that the fat fashion guy would be at this big event. We was to follow him home when he left. We did that and as the fat one got out of his car, Keller went right up behind him and then also stuck him with a needle that knocked him right out."

"Did either of you commit this murder?" Troy pointed to the photos of the dead men.

Flynn just shook his head, "No."

Overton still had more to say: "No! We put him in Flynn's car and drove to the house where you found the body. That's what Keller told us to do. The three of us snuck into the backyard by the pool. That's where we undressed him, stuffed him in that gown, and then the doctor strangled him with a strange looking rope. He also gave me an instrument to stab him in the neck. He sure bled a lot. Man, I don't know how many ways he wanted to kill this guy. Keller seemed so angry the whole time. Before Keller left, he told us to take and hide the clothes the murdered guy was wearing. Then, we should get out of there as soon as we finished doing what he asked."

"Did anyone from the house see or hear you?" Troy raised his eyebrow and asked, curious why no one seemed to have noticed them.

"Not at first. Oh yeah, he also wanted a message written on the body with the polish, but I thought it would be funnier to polish the guy's nails. Patrick started to polish all of that fat-fashion guy's nails, when we heard someone opening a door by the house. So he stopped at the two thumbnails, and then we left."

"Tom, what were you doing while Patrick was polishing the victim's nails? Troy took a drink of now cold coffee and slammed the cup down.

"Hey, I thought it would be funny to 'jerk off' on the pool house." While Tom finished dressing the fat guy, I figured: What the heck? Why not? The whole situation made me sort of wired and in need of some release. Tom was furious with me."

"Then, what did you do?" Jenna asked, shaking her head. She could see they were exhausting Troy's patience—in fact, hers, too. "Did you also ransack Nora's home and leave her the threatening message?"

"Yeah, sure, the doctor gave us another thousand dollars to help him get rid of the second guy and to leave that message for her. She was causing him problems, and a problem for him about these murders was also going to be a problem for us. I'm not stupid, ya know."

No one felt the need to reply to that comment.

"Dr. Keller had us do the same thing for the second murder, only this time we took the dead guy to the doctor's wife's office. He told us he hoped it would look like she did it and hang for murder."

"And then what?" Jenna now pressing them for answers, clearly annoyed with them.

"You know the rest. Somehow you figured we were involved and came looking for us. That's why we called Nora to pick us up so she could get Patrick's car and take us to New York City. Bitch! Instead, she brought the police to us!"

Nora once again got the blame for their misdeeds as she probably had many times before. Women like Nora seemed to have trouble getting out of their own way.

For now, Patrick Flynn and Tom Overton would certainly be going to prison for a long time. Nora would probably get some sort of break for helping the authorities capture them.

Jenna later told Dave, "Chances are Nora Flynn will continue to play victim to people like her brother and boyfriend. She doesn't seem to know any other way to relate to men or have them relate to her. It's really quite sad."

***

As Jenna anticipated, Dr. Keller's lawyer blamed Nora, her boyfriend and her brother. The lawyer claimed they were blackmailing Keller. However, Keller's arrogance and sense of entitlement had finally caught up with him. The police had enough physical evidence to arrest Keller and charge him with the murders of Andre Yellen and Kevin Larson.

In court, many months later, Keller displayed some of his irrational behavior. He talked about having been betrayed and that he had a right to "settle the score" with anyone who had betrayed him. He truly believed that, those many years ago, Yellen had betrayed him not only in business, but also by letting other people buy the gown Keller had ordered to be designed exclusively for Alana and their wedding.

Over the years, he came to believe Larson and his wife betrayed him by sleeping together off and on, in fact, for a number of years.

***

There really were no winners.

The irrational thinking of Dr. Christian Keller had caused the death of two men and another two would spend years in prison. Moreover, Keller was certainly not likely to ever again see life outside of prison.

Dr. Alana Keller, however, was not under arrest. She was only guilty of believing Yellen's and Larson's lies. They had convinced her she was as exciting and beautiful as some of the arm candy in The Hamptons.

Alana had also admitted that the argument at the Oyster Bar was Larson telling her that the idea of his putting her in one of his films was ridiculous. That was all a lie intended to piss off her husband.

Embarrassed and without husband or lovers, for now, Dr. Alana Christian, closed her East End practice and left The Hamptons.

"You know, Troy," Jenna was walking through town with him and Watson, "I keep wanting to find a rational reason for what these people did, how they acted."

"Sorry Jenna. There is none, not for them, not for anyone who wants to do so much harm others."

With his tail wagging, Watson looked at Jenna.

He seemed to agree!

CHAPTER 20

WHAT MATTERS!

With the latest murder case solved, Jenna knew she should pay more attention to Dave and the possibility of marriage, especially facing her own demons about the institution. After all, who knew when the next murder would happen in The Hamptons?

There were life experiences that framed Jenna's decisions and motivated her passions and pursuit of justice: justice denied in some ways to her grandmother; and to her friend, someone she had loved dearly, who had committed suicide.

***

Something about these murders made Jenna think about her grandmother, especially the story she had told Jenna many years ago and the promise Jenna made to her.

Jenna's grandmother grew up one of seven children in a small town in southern Italy. Jenna couldn't even remember the name of it. She had been told this story when she was 16. "Come visit me soon," her grandmother left her a phone message. This was so unlike her that Jenna called back and said she would be there the next day. There, meaning her grandmother's home in Brooklyn.

"I want you to know this darling," began her grandmother, "so you will always be careful, always protect yourself, because there are some very bad people in the world. They have no heart and they only want to satisfy their own needs, their own hungers. They don't believe in justice for anyone but themselves. They believe their behavior is justified by some unknown deity that has deemed them above the laws of moral decency. With this irrational reasoning, they live without any moral code."

Jenna was silent, mystified at the intensity of the words of her grandmother as she sat up straight in her favorite high-back, deep-blue, soft-cushion chair. They were in her grandmother's three-bedroom pre-war apartment in a high-rise building in Brooklyn, New York. Her grandmother had lived there for the past forty years, as long as Jenna had known her.

Before that, both of Jenna's grandparents had lived in a row house in another part of Brooklyn. Her grandfather was six years older than who he described as, "the love of my life forever." They were married for 58 years when he passed away at the age of 82. He was also a wonderful father. Other women would say to their husbands, "Why can't you be more like Vincent?"

Jenna's parents had wanted to move their mother to a brand-new senior facility in Manhattan, but she refused. Grandmother was stubborn to the core, which was a trait Jenna thought she had inherited.

Grandma Leena came to America to marry Vincent when she was 18. They had met a year earlier when he was visiting his own grandparents, who had lived nearby her family in Italy. They talked, had dinner with each other's families, walked along small country roads and fell in love.

Vincent promised to bring Leena to America; she promised to come to America. And they kept their promises!

"We had a very intimate ceremony with his family, went on a three-day honeymoon, stayed in a small inn surrounded by trees and mountains in upstate New York, and quickly started our family. Within the first seven years, we had five children, two boys and three girls. "Then, I told Vincent, 'Enough!' He knew I was serious when I said enough," her grandmother told her.

Jenna had heard all of this when she was younger. It was part of the family lore. It's history.

"Over the years, I became fluent in English and eventually went to school to became a teacher," Leena told Jenna.

"You lived a full life, Grandma, without any drama. You were always the smart one, the wise one and the loving one."

Jenna always felt there was something hidden, some deep secret no one might ever learn. If you asked Jenna what it was that made her feel that way, she would shake her head or shrug her shoulders. She couldn't identify where the feeling came from; but it was there, somewhat deep inside her. She and her grandmother had a strong bond. Jenna decided that the feeling might come from nothing more than that. Maybe.

Of all the family, Jenna was closest to her grandmother, perhaps because Jenna looked a lot like her. Their minds worked the same way when figuring out a problem. Besides, they both loved the old black and white movies with glamorous stars. They adored the old movie mystery series like the *Thin Man* and *Charlie Chan*.

"It was fun sharing an interest in crime and mayhem," Jenna remembered.

The two had shared books and rented mystery films that they watched together while eating popcorn, popped in the microwave. Recently, Jenna considered how these must have influenced her life and stirred her enthusiasm for being first a journalist, then a private investigator.

As a reporter, Jenna realized she had a strong ambition to seek and to tell the truth to her readers. As a private investigator, she strived to find the truth of wrongdoings and to make a difference where people had been hurt emotionally or financially—or, of course, murdered.

***

Grandma Leena, now 86, continued to sit, quite still, in her favorite chair. Her grey hair was pulled back in a bun, the way she always wore it, and she was wearing her favorite pale-pink bathrobe, which Jenna had given her as a birthday gift one year. However, her deep green eyes were filled with sadness.

Worried, Jenna said, "What is it you want to talk to me about? Are you sick? Do you need money? How can I help you? You know, I love you. I love you very much."

"Jenna," began her grandmother, "I have silent memories. I have endured a lifetime of silence with a secret that haunts me and makes me worried about you. I see how adventurous you are, living alone, and the risks you take. I watch television and hear about all the terrible things bad people do to good people, how innocence is damaged by cruelty and how a life can be changed in a moment ... like mine was."

Now, Jenna sat stunned with her own silence as her grandmother continued telling her story.

"The small town in Italy where I grew up, families expected their children would marry one another, their children would have their own children, marrying each other from one generation and then on to the next. My own parents expected I would marry a nearby neighbor's son. So did he, as did his parents."

"This boy and I were in our last year of high school together, each of us 18 years old. Then, I met your grandfather. It really was love at first sight for both of us, but we knew it would be difficult to convince my family to let me move to America and marry him. Naïve and in youthful love, I never expected there to be so much anger from the neighbor's family, especially the son."

Grandma Leena stopped and sat still as if she might not be able to continue. Jenna looked at her, took her hand and squeezed it, letting her know it was okay to tell her story.

"The son," she began again, "was known as a bully in school, but he was always nice to me, so I was surprised and very scared when I saw how angry he was. I tried to stay away from him, walked home with friends, and I even stayed home at night."

"It's okay, Grandma, I want you to tell me."

"One day, on my way home from school, he asked if he could please talk to me because he had something he wanted to tell me. I felt at the very least I owed him that much. As we walked past a small park, he pulled me into it. He hit me, threw me on the ground and raped me. I screamed for him to stop, to let me go, and he refused, saying 'Now, you'll have to marry me.' My heart still aches when I remember that experience."

Grandma continued: "I ran home with my dress all torn. My parents saw I was crying and frightened. I told them what happened. My father never said a word to me, got up and went out. Sometime later, my mother told me that he had gone to the boy's house. My father had a gun with him, which thank goodness he didn't use, but he did threaten the boy and his family."

Jenna got up to bring her grandmother a glass of water and saw her hands were shaking. When she handed the glass to her, Jenna noticed that Leena was very still in her chair. It seemed that if she moved, she would not be able to continue.

"It's okay Grandma," Jenna said, "I'm glad you told me. I'm glad you trust me."

"Jenna, there's more."

"More?"

"Yes, there's more to tell you. The boy who raped me was sent away. However, my parents were still furious, his parents were ashamed at his awful behavior . . . and me . . . I became pregnant."

The word pregnant hung in the air between Jenna and her grandmother. It carried with it all sorts of meanings and explanations. Jenna had never known what painful memories her grandmother carried around.

Grandma Leena began again, this time, with tears on her cheeks that had been wrinkled from age. "I was planning on going to America after I graduated from high school, and Vincent and I were to be married. We were so excited. When this happened, my family and I didn't know what to do. Finally, my father thought it was only right to call Vincent. He would be honest with him and tell him what happened so he would understand why I was not going to meet him and marry him."

"What changed that?" asked Jenna, softly, tenderly.

"Vincent. Vincent and his parents changed it. He came back to Italy a few weeks later to take me to America. He had a return ticket for himself and a one-way ticket for me. His family had bought them for us. They weren't very wealthy, but they owned their own business and were comfortable, a term I would come to understand.

"As Vincent held me, he promised my parents that he would always love and take care of me. He said that he would treat the child to be born as if it was his own. He believed in God and that there was a purpose to this child's life. Jenna, you are the only one other than your grandfather—and my parents who died long ago in Italy—who know this truth. That child is your father. He does not know, and he is never to know."

Jenna, not sure what to say or ask, finally said, "And then what happened?"

"We were married a few weeks after we arrived together in America. I was almost six weeks pregnant. When your father was born, we said I had a premature birth. As our first son, he was named after your grandfather's own father. We never discussed what happened in Italy. We silently agreed that our lives had begun together here in America."

Jenna got up and put her arms around her grandmother. Together they cried for a long time.

Before Jenna left that day, she made that promise to her grandmother. Softly, she said, "Grandma, I do promise to keep this secret. I promise to be careful who I trust my heart to and, share my life with. And I promise you . . . I will keep my word."

Six weeks later, Jenna's grandmother passed away of natural causes. That's what the doctor said, but Jenna thought she was ready to be with Vincent now that she had revealed her secret. Jenna's parents said they were surprised how peaceful she looked.

Jenna understood. Except she came to realize she was left with this secret that became a burden, it became a voice affecting her trust for others.

One day I'm going to have to deal with this. One day!

***

Over the years, after the loss of Jenna's own young love, she was very cautious about whom she allowed close to her. She watched others take the risk and get married; she saw good people make bad decisions because of loneliness and the perceived need to get out of their parents' homes for fear they would always be alone.

Jenna did not share those fears.

Now, Dave has found his way into her heart—and soul.

"Grandma, I think you would approve."

One day, Jenna read Dave the suicide note that Benjamin had left for her. "I was thirty, when I read it. Benjamin and I would speak almost every night. We laughed, revealed feelings and shared dreams. Then, one night he didn't call. I tried calling him and there was no answer. The next morning my phone rang, so I thought it might be him."

Jenna, it's Benjamin's brother, "He's dead! He took his own life. He left a note for you."

"I remember him sobbing and my saying with disbelief, "It can't be. It must be someone else." Yet, something told me, of course it's him. He too had kept a secret that he couldn't live with any longer."

Weeks later, Benjamin's brother brought the note to her. They cried together. She put the note away until she was ready to read it. After that, she never saw him or any of his family ever again.

Accepting the wisdom of Kabbalah eventually helped Jenna accept that a young man she loved—who she thought had loved her—had taken his own life at age twenty-three. She was only nineteen.

Benjamin had written that note to her and left it in a sealed envelope. She did not open it until her thirtieth birthday. After having found a life of happiness living in The Hamptons, she knew she could handle whatever it said.

Still, the secrets within became her burden.

***

Stunned by her grandmother's story and the loss of her own young love, Jenna had felt driven to explore Kabbalah. The study of this ancient wisdom and knowledge with an incredible teacher helped her to find her own truths.

In college, while studying journalism at Columbia University, Jenna had seen a flyer about a Kabbalah lecture. It fascinated her with its simple message: *"Free Kabbalah lecture. Explore the meaning of life. Your life!"*

The flyer gave the time, date and place. She got there early so she could ask the lecturer, "I'm not Jewish. Does that matter?" Welcoming her, the lecturer responded, "Wisdom and knowledge is for everyone. I hope you'll stay."

Stay she did.

For the next eight years, Jenna went to many lectures on Kabbalah. She also had private conversations and read some of the most insightful books on the subject under the guidance of a learned rabbi.

Jenna and the rabbi became friends. They discussed religion, psychology and philosophy of human behavior. They explored the value of "Socratic Questioning." The rabbi explained: "It's a way of getting to the truth of the matter. You can bring this into any part of your life, work, friendship and even love."

In a private session, Jenna asked the question haunting her for so long, "Why had Benjamin committed suicide?"

"Perhaps he was driven by emotions that made him believe he could not change the pain he was feeling. He believed he could no longer tolerate it or stop what was causing it. Your greatest gift to him, and to yourself, would be to forgive him. I hope someday you'll open the note you told me he left you."

When she did, she truly forgave Benjamin. She finally understood.

***

Dear Jenna,

My heart breaks to write you, knowing yours will ache, because we will have both lost a dream we had. I know yours was for us to be together. Mine was not. Not romantically. I have known for many years that I am gay. I have never told anyone. So many fears stopped me. My parents never would have accepted this and to live a lie any longer is intolerable for me. I pray you will one day forgive me and understand what must seem like a cowardly way out.

I am safe, in a better place. I do love you.

Love,
Benjamin

CHAPTER 21

CASE CLOSED

Dr. Gold had described irrational behavior: "It is one of the most difficult behaviors to deal with. When someone is being irrational, they don't listen to reason, logic or even common sense. They are unpredictable and sometimes even dangerous. In fact, they can snap at any time."

The individuals involved in causing Yellen and Larson's murders had all acted irrationally.

Nora just wanted to be loved. It didn't seem to matter who it was.

Nora's brother and boyfriend wanted to have money without working for it, and it didn't matter what they had to do to get it.

Dr. Christian Keller believed he had the right to seek and exact revenge, and it didn't matter that he was taking two lives.

***

Patricia wrote a two-page article with photos that appeared in the local daily paper. The headline read: "Fashion Queen and Movie Mogul Murderers Arrested." It recounted the whole story with its sordid details of the people involved, the murders, and how the murderers were captured.

The national press blazed similar headlines: "The Hamptons 'Fashion Queen' and 'Movie Mogul' Murderers Caught."

Most of the media sensationalized it—but nothing like the gossip papers with all sorts of photos showing Yellen and Larson in compromising positions and both of the Kellers looking like criminals, which was definitely not a good look for either of them!

The twenty-four hour television news showed photos of the two murdered men, a reporter standing outside of Larson's home. The headline for this report: "Fashion Queen and Lover Pay High Price for Beauty in the Fashionable Hamptons." This was followed by an overview of the murders, a few more location shots and on to the next story.

The local weekly rags ran photos of the celebrities who were murdered under the headline: "Beauty Fades Out... Movie Mogul and Fashion Queen Lover Dead in The Hamptons." A couple of them also further sensationalized their story with photos and quotes from locals who had worked for them in past years.

Jenna's favorite headline was: "Dr. Christian Keller, Famed Hampton Cosmetic Surgeon, Needs Nose Job!" He had been hurt during the murder case.

***

On the front page of the second section was a photo of the rescued golden retriever who had been tied to the fence, company name prominently behind it, with the caption, "Retriever Died of Cruel Treatment."

"Dr. Dave Carter, a popular local veterinarian whose family has lived out here for nearly 200 years called the paper and provided photos he obtained from a couple who found the dog and brought it to him. "I can promise this firm and others like them will be held accountable for their actions and treatment of these dogs. I don't care if these companies support our senator; they are also supporting cruelty to these animals by allowing this to happen. My center will be glad to take in dogs for free when people leave at the end of the season. How difficult can it be for someone to drop the dogs off here? No questions asked."

The reporter went on to write, "We contacted the business where the dog was found tied and Senator Quinn for a response to Dr. Carter. Both refused to comment."

***

At the end of a big case, Jenna usually had dinner with Patricia, Lara and Kristin. This time, Mary Bennett joined them at the Burger Bar. Wine and special appetizers covered the table. After discussing the case and reading all the headlines, they agreed they had had their fill of talking about murder. For now, anyhow!

"You know," commented Kristin, "With so much cosmetic surgery, people are truly dying to be beautiful. It's a fact that many die each year from these surgeries. It's crazy."

"Well what about all the botched surgeries? The desire to look good is endless especially for those who summer in the Hamptons." Patricia was picking at some appetizers and drinking a glass of white wine.

"All that cosmetic surgery is nuts to me," Jenna said. "Although maybe not quite as much as the crazy behavior we've seen from the recent murders. We need to be very cautious when dealing with them. I've learned it's best not to confront them." The others nodded in agreement.

"Unless it's the senator," laughed Kristin.

"Yeah, appears Dave is taking him on," Jenna grinned holding up a glass of wine to acknowledge her pride in him.

"Well, I'd like to add my thoughts about the senator," Mary put down her drink and was very serious. "You know, he is completely unwilling to help do anything about the homeless issue out here. It's a bigger problem than most people want to admit. Lots of people are more concerned about the beauty of The Hamptons and keeping it that way. We need to try and help the homeless, even if just a little. So, starting next month, once a month, I plan to offer free lunch and maybe some other services at my bar."

The issue would become a cause for all of them.

***

Aggie was chasing after Watson, who was full of energy, running in and out of the ocean. Aggie stopped short at the water's edge while Watson's tail was wagging with joy. After all, he had helped catch a criminal!

Watson was doing his best to drag Jenna and Dave with him into the water, although not successfully.

The sun was setting and a beautiful Hampton moon was rising, getting ready to face the ocean. They were enjoying the beach, Dave and Jenna with the Irish setters.

Jenna was uncharacteristically quiet. Tomorrow, she was leaving for the city.

"It's time. I need to escape to the city," Jenna told Dave the day after the recent murder case had been solved. That was almost a week ago.

"I'm going to spend the next few weeks in Manhattan. It's a wonderful time to be there with far less traffic. It's fun to sit outside at cafés, visit great flea markets throughout the city and watch outdoor dancing at Lincoln Center. Just thinking about it makes me happy!"

Dave thought she sounded like she was trying too hard to convince him and herself. He agreed to keep Watson and Aggie at *The Farm*. Troy promised he would pray for no murders to interrupt her.

James agreed to take care of investigating several of her smaller insurance fraud cases. "You can call or email me if you have any questions or problems with them."

As she handed James the paperwork for the cases, Jenna reached over and gave him a hug.

James was leaning against the fence around the Irish setters' play area at Dave's. He knew he had found a special, new family.

Dave understood Jenna's need "to escape," as she called it. Soon fall would be arriving in The Hamptons, but in the meantime, the summer crazies were in rare form with wild parties, big events and major traffic buildups going east.

Jenna's parents were thrilled to have their daughter and only child spend some time with them, even though they would be away for one of the weeks she was there.

What Jenna hadn't told Dave, or anyone, was her main reason for going to the city. She had decided to see Dr. Gold for personal reasons.

We all have secrets, she thought. They can undermine our happiness. The voices of the past are haunting my life, keeping me from marrying a man I love. It's time to deal with them, to get rid of them! Including Raace Scanlon.

M. Glenda Rosen

"Dying To Be Beautiful"
Mystery Series
Dying to be Beautiful... Without A Head, February 1, 2016
Dying to be Beautiful... Fashion Queen, Spring, 2016

In The Works
Dying To Be Beautiful... Fake Beauty
Dying To Be Beautiful... Skin Deep

A Huge Thanks To:
Dita Dow, Advisor
Former Albuquerque, New Mexico, Police Detective
Founder: Black Horse Private Investigations

And
My Editor and Friend,
Janice Artandi

Books by Marcia G. Rosen (M. Glenda Rosen)
The Woman's Business Therapist
My Memoir Workbook
Living An Illuminated Life (iBook)

www.creativebookconcepts.com

Member: Public Safety Writers Association
The Private Eye Writers of America (PWA)
Sisters in Crime: National, San Francisco and Los Angeles
Greater Los Angeles Writers Society
Malice Domestic
PULSE, NY

Another....

Dying To Be Beautiful
Mystery
'Fake Beauty'

By

M. Glenda Rosen

Thursday, 8am

Author of best selling book, "Looking Beautiful" wasn't looking so beautiful.

Jordan Kennedy was found stuffed into the window of the local bookstore.

The bookstore was now on fire with Jordan Kennedy looking like a dead Raggedy Ann doll, tossed on top of copies of her books beginning to burn.

Posters of her book signing scheduled for the coming Saturday had been plastered throughout The Hamptons for the past several weeks, many of them now had a huge red X scratched across them.

Someone watching the fire looked very familiar to Jenna Preston.

"There's no end to people *Dying to be Beautiful in The Hamptons.*

CHAPTER 1

AUTHOR IN THE WINDOW

"What the hell?

Jenna literally gasped as she noticed Michael Preston, her father's brother, standing across the street, watching the fire and murder scene unfold. Raace Scanlon standing on his left turned to whisper something to him.

Many years ago Jenna had a brief falling into bed with Raace. It ended almost as quickly as it began, and yet after all these years her heart skipped a beat when she saw him, but that was more out of concern from things they had talked about during one long passionate night of love making. After a few more times together it was over, and they had remained friendly. Nothing more. Youthful experiences bring memories of their own and seeing him stirred those memories...and concerns.

***

The Hamptons had changed...a lot

Over the last twenty years, more and more of the wealthy landed on its shores building homes of excessive size, bringing along excessive demands for whatever it is they wanted and well, it seemed that this excess also brought along more crime and murders.

Each year and each season the beauty of The Hamptons that stretches across the south shore of the far-east end of Long Island, with growing vineyards the north shore, quite unwillingly opened it's doors to the wealthy.

Hampton local, meant you were native born to the area, or lived here for at least fifty years. Some stay and shake their heads in dismay. Some stay and make a lot of money off the summer intruders. Some sell and move to a place where they perceive, or at least hope, there could perhaps be a better quality of life for them.

It was an odd and mixed sense of reality, myth and wishful thinking. It was hard to believe someone would want to cause such damage in the Hamptons which held so much pride about its beauty.

Yet the ringing of fire engines, police cars blaring their sirens and the acid smell of smoke billowing upwards from the fire were all warning signs to get out of the way.

To stay out of the way of danger.

Jenna's Irish Setter Watson was not keen on heeding the warnings

"Watson hold on," shouted Jenna, as her red flowery wide brim hat she was wearing flew behind her almost onto Aggie.

Watson, his red hair and tail flying in front of her, was dragging Jenna towards the fire, as the much smaller puppy, Aggie, whimpering, was being carried by Dave. The smell of smoke was already filling the air and the quiet early fall morning was turning into chaos. Onlookers were gathering across the street from the bookstore becoming engulfed in flames.

"Dave, can you get Watson, I see Troy's car, this had to be more than a fire. Also if possible collect my hat, please."

Watson continued to pull Jenna towards the chaos. Watson, it seemed, had a nose for murder!

There *was* a murder, and ultimately much more. Including a dangerous situation at 'the farm', owned by Dave.

Dave her present love, well really, her hot romance, a Veterinarian, also raised Setters at 'the farm'.

They first met when she went to buy Watson a few years ago.

Dave, like Detective Troy Johnson, Jenna's partner in crime solving, was a local, born and raised on the north fork, on farmland. They and their families before them had a history with this land. Taking good care of it mattered to them...a lot.

Even Jenna Preston, was considered a newcomer, having lived out here for *only a little over* twenty years. Long red hair, blue eyes, nearly 5'5", her Irish Setter, Watson often by her side. She was attempting to dismiss her own demons stopping her from marrying this man she loved. Demons a psychiatrist in New York and she had explored since the past summer.

***

Dave holding on tight to Aggie, grabbed Watson's leash from Jenna, then knelt down and gently stroked his head to calm him for fear he was going to pull loose and tear through town. For some reason he was very spooked by what was happening.

Sergeant Stan Miller was pushing back onlookers, forcing several people to move out of the street and stopping the media from rushing towards the building in efforts to take photos.

Jenna stood staring, watching the fire department as they began breaking through the front window of the bookstore. Two fire trucks and the chief were there as flames seem to grow with intensity.... quickly and violently.

A third fire truck was on the way to the scene from one of the neighboring communities, more sirens blasting through the fall morning.

Easily a three-alarm fire, with flames eagerly jumping from the backdoor throughout the two-story bookstore located at the edge of town. The whole block would eventually have to be sealed off as a crime scene.

Inside the front window Jenna saw books sprawled all over, some ripped, some tossed on top of a very dead woman. She realized this was the woman she had met at a luncheon the day before.

The fire suddenly blasted into the front of the bookstore, where the popular author had been spread out in the window, with a huge red X across her face. Before she had been pulled out of the window Jenna noticed that on top of her body was a copy of the popular children's book, *The Beauty and The Beast.*"

Two of the fireman had pulled her out, then handed her to Detective Johnson and Sergeant Miller who quickly carried her away from the building.

Within a few more minutes the fire exploded from the back to the front of the bookstore with a noise that rocked the small village for blocks. More people started coming out of their homes, those who lived nearby heard the fire engines and smelled the smoke as the explosion tore through the village with a scary and fierce intensity.

"I'm going to arrest the whole goddamn lot of you who are trying to get photos. Get out of our way," Sergeant Miller grabbed one of the guys by the elbow, walking him to the other side of the street, quietly whispering, Zack, email those photos to me."

Zack ever so slightly nodded yes, he and Miller had helped each other like this for many years. After hours they were drinking and card playing buddies.

Other photographers shouting.

"Hey just let us get a couple photos of the dead lady."

"Yeah, we're just doing our job."

"Troy we have to get her body out of here." Miller yelled as he maneuver the gawkers.

"Doc Bishop will be here any minute, grab the blanket from trunk of my police car.

Blake Wilson, owner of the bookstore was standing in the middle of the street hysterical, screaming, "Put out the damn fire, what the hell are you doing?"

Detective Johnson shoved him out of the street and seeing Jenna waved her over, told her who he was.

"Jenna, best to take Blake to the police station. Miller and I have to take care of the crime scene, the body, and talk to Chief Bradley about the fire. As we took the body from him he yelled to me, "I smelled an accelerant which was most likely what was used to start the fire. I'll have my investigator check it out and meet up with you and your forensic people in a few hours."

"Ok, we'll meet you back at the police station"

"Thanks. Doc Bishop will take the body back to the morgue and we'll get Lara Stern started on forensic investigation as soon as she can get near the building, it's too hot now."

Jenna heard Doc who arrived minutes before yell to his intern, "Common let's her into the van. Now!"

The fire chief was shouting, "Everyone move, the building is about to collapse, the fire has spread throughout the entire structure!"

***

Fall had arrived in The Hamptons with soft, slightly cooler breezes off the ocean that felt glorious after the heat and humidity of a Long Island summer. Acres of pumpkins, corn, and fall flowers dressed the landscape.

Best of all for those who lived here year round, many of the summer residents had packed up their bathing suits, fancy cars and left with their egos and arrogance.

The East End was still busy, active, but traffic no longer dominated the highways or felt as if it was threatening to life and limb when crossing the streets.

It would be foolish to believe The Hamptons became a version of Xanadu because of the calendar change and shorter days.

If that was the case there would not be, what was apparently another murder.